Books by William Lychack:

The Wasp Eater

The Architect of Flowers

Cargill Falls

Cargill Falls

CARGILL FALLS

a novel

WILLIAM LYCHACK

Cargill Falls. Copyright 2020 by William Lychack. All rights reserved. No part of this book may be reproduced in any form or by any electronic or mechanical means, or the facilitation thereof, including information storage and retrieval systems, without permission in writing from the publisher, except by a reviewer who may quote brief passages in a review. Any members of educational institutions wishing to photocopy part or all of the work for classroom use, or publishers who would like to obtain permission to include the work in an anthology, should send their inquiries to braddockavenue@gmail.com.

This is a work of fiction. Names, characters, places, and incidents are either the product of imagination or are used fictitiously. Any resemblance to actual persons, events, or locales is entirely coincidental.

Excerpts of this novel have appeared in *Story Magazine, Washington Square Review, Conjunctions, The Idaho Review, The Forge Literary Review, Waxwing, Coal Hill Review, The Laurel Review, The Fourth River Review,* and the *North American Review.* The author would like to thank the editors of these magazines, especially Spencer Gaffney, Michael Nye, Bradford Morrow, Christine Stroud, John Haggerty, Yosh Haggerty, and Mitch Wieland. Appreciation goes also to the National Endowment for the Arts, the Corporation of Yaddo, the Sherwood Anderson Foundation, the Christopher Isherwood Foundation, the Heinz Endowments, the Pittsburgh Foundation, the Sewanee Writers' Conference, and the Writing Program at the University of Pittsburgh.

Printed in the United States of America
10 9 8 7 6 5 4 3 2 1

FIRST EDITION, February 2020

ISBN 10: 1-7328956-5-2
ISBN 13: 978-1-7328956-5-2

Cover design by Denise McMorrow
Book design by Savannah Adams

Braddock Avenue Books
P.O. Box 502
Braddock, PA 15104

www.braddockavenuebooks.com

Braddock Avenue Books is distributed by Small Press Distribution.

For Charles Baxter

To fly and breathe in the air may be better than to swim and breathe in the water; but if the fins of a fish aimed at converting themselves into wings, the fish, as a fish, would perish.

—MIGUEL DE UNAMUNO,
TRAGIC SENSE OF LIFE

CARGILL FALLS

—PART ONE—

— I —

We once found a gun in the woods—true story—me and Brownie, two of us walking home from school one day, twelve years old, and there on the ground in the leaves was a pistol. Almost didn't even notice. Almost passed completely by. Had to be the last thing we expected, gun all black and dull at our feet, Brownie almost kicking it aside like an empty bottle or little-kid toy.

But then we saw what it was for real and got those shit-eating grins on our faces. We looked back to make sure no one else was coming. Nothing but skinny trees and muddy trail in either direction. Not even a bird chirping that we could hear. We held our breath to listen, everything so quiet we were afraid to move, whole world teetering as if balanced on a point.

Late winter, early spring, and we picked whatever leaves and twigs from around the gun. We made a little nest for the thing, neither of us saying a word. No shine to the metal at all. No trace of kindness anywhere in this object. Just sharp lines and hard edges.

Soon we were poking it with sticks. We hunched close to read the stamp on the barrel—COLT, GOVERNMENT, CALIBER .45—like we had any idea what any of this meant. We were just kids, Brownie a big romp of a boy with straight-across bangs and face full of freckles, and this Mouse character—me—standing alongside with my ears and toothy smirk, the two of us there in the middle of the woods with a gun.

What could go wrong?

Brownie pulled his hand into his sleeve and slowly lifted the pistol as if from out of a fire. He dangled the gun in front of me by the handle. It seemed to absorb the light in a way that made me feel bad for us.

We were doomed.

We didn't stand a chance.

"This," said Brownie, "is seriously real."

And still those dopey grins to each other—him and me in total cahoots—as if already we were permanently linked by whatever this was going to be. Some part of us must have liked the idea of danger, the feeling of fear and power in our lives. In some way we must have wanted to make the gun a story we could tell about ourselves. Good or bad, great or small, it felt like a spell we were under, Brownie going back and forth with the gun, waving it slow and steady under my nose.

"Let me see it," I told him.

I stood with my hand open and waited until he stopped and lowered the gun to me. My arm tugged down with the weight, that solidness so much more satisfying than anyone could have ever explained. The diamond ridges of the grip, the fit just so perfect in the hand.

Without thinking I pointed the gun at Brownie—at his chest, my finger curling over the trigger—and he put up his hands and said don't shoot.

"I'm innocent!" he said.

"Gimme the cash," I told him.

"Okay, okay," he said and made like he was counting out money. I waved for him to hurry along. Should have been funny, the old bank robber routine, the flustered clerk, the wag of gunpoint, seen it a hundred times.

Years from this place—a lifetime away from these boys—and still I can't help but wish I could reach down and somehow lift the gun away from these two little idiots. Give them baseball practice or trumpet lessons. Somehow linger them back to the playground after school with friends. Wish I could make a nice little train set of their town: Cargill Falls, Connecticut, circa 1980, its old mills and tired little worker houses, its churches and sidewalks and cemeteries, the grocery and package stores, that constant hint of potato chips in the air from the Frito-Lay factory in the next town over. If I could, I'd put these boys anywhere but the woods that day. I'd set them out by the train station, figurines throwing rocks at the freight cars going by. I'd get them out near the river where the carp pucker the weeds above the falls. I'd wander them home through a kind of Busytown, give them bikes to ride, whisper down for them to get out of here already. That'd be me rustling the maple and oak leaves, just enough to spook these kids away.

Not like they'd have listened, of course. Not like they'd have been able to hear a single word. All the iron filings would line up on that magnet of a gun for them, and yet there were still so many things a pair of boys might have done different at this point in the story. We could have gone straight to the police. We could have swaddled the pistol to leave on the steps of the fire station. We could have called my mother at the department store where she worked. She'd be in PETS or TOYS or CUSTOMER SERVICE near the back. They'd have to page her over the intercom. She'd need to make her way past the registers with this fear growing in her that the worst had happened. We could turn that fear of hers into something tangible, something more than just credit for being good. We could use the gun to get something, something equal to the relief she'd feel when she knew we were safe.

Mrs. Brownell worked at the front desk of the middle school. Every day she sat stern and impassible, dealing with kids in trouble. If we went to her, she'd know just by the looks on our faces. "What's the matter?" she'd ask.

She'd stand and lead us to an empty classroom, where we could be heroes.

Yet with this raw weight and power in our hands, the fit of the gun so perfect, we must have no longer wished to be smart or nice anymore.

We wanted to *use* the gun.

We needed to *shoot* something.

It was as *plain* and *obvious* and *stupid* as that.

For whatever reason, it seemed a thing required: the two of us must have needed to make what everyone would think was the exact wrong decision. Otherwise we'd have long since started for Brownie's father at CL&P—Connecticut Light and Power—the two of us finding Mr. Brownell in one of the big maintenance stations, man up to his elbows in some kind of engine or generator.

We'd have approached all timid and shy, awed by this half-dim cathedral of machinery. He'd be annoyed at first, interrupted at work, saying, "This better be good."

But then he'd have been so proud when we showed what we found, when he realized what we'd done by coming to him. Such an obvious triumph it would have been, though we must not have wanted to shine in any such way, because we never went anywhere near the power company that afternoon, never went looking for him down at the Elks or the Knights of Columbus or wherever else it was he wound up this time of day. We didn't wait at the top of Addison Street. He'd have arrived to us sooner or later, that rattle of utility truck in the dusk, Brownie's father coming home, pulling up to the curb, saying, "What are you two numbnuts doing out here?"

— 2 —

Brownie was large and loud and funny, whereas I was small and quiet and hardly ever funny at all. Nothing humorous about a Mouse, really, but still Brownie laughed when I aimed the gun at him. I went big for a moment and asked what was so hilarious. And when he didn't answer, I raised the pistol from his chest to his face to help him hear the question better. He knew I wouldn't do anything and smiled and shook his head sadly at me. He slid himself away from the line of where a bullet would go.

I hated him standing there all sane and sensible, though I also loved him being realistic and mature. If Brownie stayed calm and responsible, then I had every permission in the world to be dumb and crazy. We had this balance-of-the-universe thing between us. If he went high road, then it was up to me to take us low, him asking if I would just please move my finger off the trigger, him suggesting I should point the gun away.

Clearly there were rules to all of this. Finding the gun meant we could not go home until we fired the thing. It was my turn to pull the slide the way I had seen on television. I tried not to show how scared I was. I tried to make it look easy. I pressed the front sight, the rear sight, tried prying open the handle. Looking down the hole of the muzzle was like leaning over the mouth of a well. The same lurch of stomach. The same dark pull going all the way down. I could feel the metal of the gun crawling up my arm, the malice of it seeping into me. And from the woods we could hear the late buses riding out from school. I went to one knee and put the gun back in its little cradle of leaves, tucking it in for the night, blowing warm air into my fists as I stood.

"We can't just leave it like that," said Brownie—such patience he had for me sometimes. He poked the handle with the toe of his shoe. "I mean, what if some little kid comes along and finds it?"

"We can bury it," I told him.

I could tell he needed me to be more rational, and I tried saying how no one would find anything after we were done.

"What if they end up hurting themselves?" he asked. "How would you feel then?"

I told him I wouldn't care at all. I said that I meant it, too, from the bottom of my heart, my voice going desperate and thin. It was the voice of a weasel, and Brownie looked back along the trail, as if it'd be embarrassing to be seen out here, brainless and bickering.

He said it had my fingerprints on it now, and I told him we could wipe them off. I picked the gun from the leaves and began rubbing the handle along the front of my coat. I kept pushing the barrel over the length of my thigh, as if trying to conjure a genie, Brownie edging closer, saying to be careful. Be pretty dumb to shoot ourselves by accident.

He lifted the gun out of my hand, and I started to drift away. Such lightness I felt without the pistol, Brownie back to being Brownie, saying "Stand back, little fella, and watch how it's done."

There would be nothing to worry about as long as we stuck to the script, as long as we stayed true to who we were supposed to be in the world. But still sometimes it wasn't pretty, being Mouse, forever nervous and nibbling at the edges of things, always scavenging bits and scraps. In Little League, Mouse would be exiled to right field, where they sent boys to go daydream and be all Pisces by nature (timid, wishy-washy, full of doubt).

The complete antithesis would be catcher, like Brownie, where you had to be rugged and smart. It helped to have a cannon for an arm, like he did, Brownie hitting cleanup, slouching in his muscles, pudgy and tough little Libra (gritty, bit of a scamp, not scared to stay down on a ball). Mouse would have no arm to speak of, no glove skills, no father, no little brother, no paper route, not even a dog waiting at home for him. Mouse had no sly glance to try to melt anyone's heart, no youth hockey on weekends, no cottage on a lake a few towns over, no motorboat, no water skiing.

It only made sense that Brownie would end up with the gun, his hands so much more suited for the job. Brownie's fingers were thick and scabbed from cutting wood with his father, grease worked into the knuckles and fingernails. The hands of Mouse were soft and pale. Like he was afraid to touch things in the world, like he was saving himself for something.

• • •

    Inside the quiet of the woods that day, there with the gun after school, a strange hush of leaves closed in on us, branches and trunks stretching, trees creaking like ropes. Brownie and I looked at each other. Were those voices? Were we starting to hear things now?

    A girl laughing—faint gusts of music—and then the steady splashing of feet through the leaves, the gradual *shush, shush, shush* of someone marching toward us.

    Brownie put his hands into his jacket pockets slow and lawful, gun like a little boner poking. Ribbons of voices and laughter carried past where we stood. I looked down to make sure I wasn't holding anything. I literally raised my hands to my eyes like a crazy person, like I didn't trust my own fingers to be empty. Nothing but naked palms and fortune-teller lines, and those footsteps approaching, Brownie turning to watch where the path lined up, the two of us waiting for our first victims to appear.

— 3 —

Funny we just stood there—could have run, could have hidden, could have turned into different kinds of kids—Brownie with his fists deep in his pockets, me standing steadfast and loyal beside him.

He nudged my shoulder when they appeared. Two guys, two girls, the four of them on the path in front of us. High school kids. One had a cigarette, smoke trailing behind like a veil. They were older, talking and laughing, totally oblivious in the woods, disrespectful to the place, the trees, the path. And maybe Brownie and I blended in so well that we weren't even there anymore. Anything seemed possible—none of them noticing us waiting completely still, me with my knees shivering from the cold, Brownie with a gun in his pocket.

They were fifty, thirty, twenty feet away, a crescendo of footsteps and leaves and voices closing in, the four of them so ignorant it seemed almost supernatural, until all at once Brownie stepped forward, the two of us materializing right in front of their eyes. Just like that, me and Brownie looming like guardians of the forest.

We must have looked ridiculous, the way they laughed so easy and automatic. Didn't move a muscle, didn't give an inch as they approached—nice little air pocket of awkward in the woods—the two of us hanging spooky and weird in front of them. They searched around our feet, as if something should be there to explain such behavior, grins coming in and out of focus on their faces, the one girl dropping her cigarette, twisting her toe over it in the leaves. The prettier of the two tried to hike a smile back to her lips.

What a wonderful thing for a pair of boys to learn: the less we moved, the more insolent and sarcastic we seemed to become. The less we seemed to care, the more menace and power we had. A kind of strength in our quiet. Maybe we shrugged our shoulders, maybe we shifted our feet, but that was the most we were going to give them. Something in us must have loved the way they went so tight and nervous. Their skin not so good close up. The pretty girl with her smile slipping again.

"Creepy little kids," she said. "Gotta love 'em."

That swerve of her voice pulled me forward slightly—some air that I wanted to hold, cigarettes and peppermint—and one of the guys laughed and called us homos. Out here cornholing each other, he said, and he leered at me and made kissy faggot sounds in my face, his breath warm and sour, teeth and tonsils. It'd be his fault now if anything bad happened. We were demons disguised as scrawny kids. They should have had some foreboding, some inkling of the harm hovering a foot or two away.

Instead they stayed so predictable. On their way to go fornicate one minute, and then blocked by two fuckhead twerps the next, the guy closest starting to take flicks at my ears. He had one of those cowboy shirts with snaps instead of buttons, and he poked my chest like I was made of tissue paper, like maybe his finger would push through.

Brownie slid a look over to me, and I forwarded the message, my eyes going silent to one couple, then silent to the other. They had to recognize that we weren't scared. They should have been wary. They should have kept their distance. Like seeing a raccoon in daylight. But still this douchebag placed his hand on my chest, the girls giggling as he shoved me back.

I went like a boat being launched—whip of saplings, crush of leaves, me falling to the ground. Brownie barely moved as I got up. I pulled the wet seat of my pants from my skin. Such restraint, such patience and power, Brownie waiting with his hands in his pockets as I took my place next to him.

"Weebles wobble," said the pretty girl.

And maybe they were high. Maybe they were drinking, the pretty girl winking at me, her boyfriend stepping up to launch me once more. But then there was Brownie moving forward. Brownie with that single crunch of leaves under his shoe.

"Don't touch him," he said.

He could have been dipped in bronze, this statue of a boy, Brownie saying, "Go around."

And how lucky for these people that it was him who had the gun. If it were me, I'd have had them cowering on the ground. Eat those leaves! Bark like a dog! I'd have stabbed the pistol into their ribs—look who's all neutered and nutless now!—but Brownie had a much bigger heart than I would ever have. That much was absolutely true. It would be his downfall. He should have been more selfish and petty (like me), more wounded and resentful and quick to think the worst (like me), less forgiving and calm and strong (like he was).

The prettier of the girls pulled at her boyfriend. "C'mon, Jimmy," she said, "let's get out of here."

Jimmy called us shitbirds and brushed past, the other couple following with that eyeball silence of theirs. Brownie clucked his tongue as they went, which was what his father would do, Mr. Brownell making that sound, that final cluck of tongue, whenever he arrived at some prime number truth. Our inability to stack a woodpile, for instance. Our uselessness in the face of any real work, for another.

We watched them go along the path, our old pal Jimmy with his hand in the back pocket of the pretty girl's jeans, a detail which made me want to harm him even more. Such an urge I had to find a rock to throw. I needed to teach him a lesson, have him chase me through the woods, get him lured into some trap of Brownie's and mine.

I kicked a stone loose from the path and threw it as hard as I could, the rock landing nowhere close to them, the couples vanishing safe and sound at the bend in the path. The woods were empty, yet there still seemed something unfinished, something hateful and mean in the bare trees, the gray sky, the sinking cold.

"Want to scare them for real?" I asked.

I took a stick and swung. I made kissy sounds and called for Jimmy. I asked if we should make them suffer, and Brownie went along for a while, though I could tell he was somewhere else in his mind. You could see him already onto the next problem—where to go? what to do?—and my nonsense only added to the weight of the gun for him.

• • •

Worse things would happen in our lives. We would *think* worse and *say* worse and *do* worse and *be* worse in the months and years to come, but the pistol was *our first worst thing*. Other kids had mothers who were worse. They had worse fathers, worse accidents happening all the time. Even small mill towns like ours had tragedies more worthy than a gun in the woods. Rodney Sellers had a babysitter put him in a clothes dryer, the skin on his arms and the backs of his hands like melted wax. The Garcia girls drowned together in Alexander's Lake. Cathy Deary died of leukemia. People wedged coins into the letters of her name in the cemetery.

The gun was nothing compared to what other kids had to deal with, but still *it was ours*. The gun was a chance, a challenge to prove who we were. And there was nothing that could have come close to equaling a pistol for us. A dead body, a suitcase full of money, a stash of booze or girlie magazines. Pound for pound, our gun was the absolute perfect thing to find—scary like an animal, scary like an urge—and we carried it in our possession back to the school with us. We peeled away from the trail, let the high school couples escape our wrath, Jimmy and his girlfriend safe for now, and we ended up on the hill overlooking the big-humped roof of the elementary school, the familiar brickwork of cafeteria and gymnasium, Brownie circling us toward the parking lot in front. We were here to check for his mother's car, that gray Cutlass meaning she was still at the front desk, which would mean his younger brother Tommy was still in the library at Little Friends, which would mean Brownie and I still had this window of time between school and dinner to survive.

We circled around toward the playground and library, that blanket of clouds over everything, a muffled quiet to the world. No one on the ballfields or basketball courts, no kids playing, which meant no getting Dave or Chubs or Moon in on this.

Somebody had clapped erasers against the wall down near the library. Either by chance or design, they'd made a phantom of chalk dust, face gazing pale and misty from the bricks—sockets, mouth—and it was just that empty desolation of brown fields and gray asphalt, his mother and brother in the school, and the two of us alone on the edge of the hill looking down.

Brownie's face seemed bruised in the light when I turned to him, his bones made of pewter under the skin. And if he had looked scared and cold to me, then what on earth must I have looked like to him? If he wasn't equal to this, then what hope could I have had?

No wonder we were so quiet—hard to risk a single word—and we turned from the school to start over again through the woods, stutter-stepping where we'd found the gun in the leaves. On the path we could see our past selves standing there, wispy little kids hovering, Brownie and I hurrying past the stonewalls, and past the brook to the public spring at the base of Wicker street.

The spring was an iron pipe. We drank the water, crisp and sweet as corn. The final buses rode back light and empty to school, children all safely home, crossing guard gone from the intersection, Providence Street and the cemetery, my house hidden beyond the far wall. We scuffed along the streets, in and out of the gutters, watching for any hint of car approaching, that shark gray of his mother's Cutlass always just about to appear.

A little ways more and we could see my house—square white box, aluminum siding, pink roof, willow trees. No

Chevelle in the driveway meant no mother home early from work, meaning no reason to stop, meaning the gun could keep pulling us through the cemetery toward the pond. We passed statues and headstones, passed Cathy under the grass with her coins, passed the brick toolshed near the end of the graves, and kept going past the gravel banks, the piles of old brush and trash out where no one could see, plastic wreaths and flowers, scrub trees, broken concrete, old tires, a refrigerator dumped like a coffin.

There were signs—NO TRESPASSING, NO DUMPING, NO HUNTING—not that we paid attention to any such things. Nothing could stop us. We walked with purpose and caught the first glimpse of water dark and glossy below.

We skated the pond in winter, and we fished it in summer, and here at the spillway we took out the gun. Still a surprise, this thing in Brownie's hand between us. The web of his thumb wrapped around that beak-curve of handle. The trigger like a quarter-moon under his finger.

"What now?" I asked.

It was a dumb question—and he rightly ignored me—because anyone with half a brain could see what had to happen next. Everything commenced from this edge of pond, pines feathering that bowl of water. In some ways they would be there forever, these two boys standing near the spillway, the water like a sheet of glass bending smooth and green over the dam, Brownie knocking that crown of the grip on the heel of his hand. There was this muffled clink of metal as he hit, and little pieces of dried earth collected in his palm. He sprinkled them over the leaves.

Some thirty years later, one of us would take his own life in a motel room, while the other would end up doing what exactly? Am I here to honor these kids? Am I trying to betray them even more? Am I just hoping to be rid of them somehow?

Who knows, but I'm riding home on a train—Pittsburgh to Harrisburg to Penn Station to Providence—hours of Pennsylvania farms and forests and little towns, an occasional barn or tree holding the eye, and I keep thinking about that gun we found as kids, as if this alone could explain everything that followed for us, including his wife, Brenda, calling with the news, saying there'd be a service at the Elks, asking if I could be there to say something for Brownie.

Ahead will be my old friends. They'll be waiting upstairs in the banquet hall of the Elks. Dave and Chubs and Moon, Liz and Jen, the usual gang at one of the tables near the windows. Brownie's mother and father will be there, as will his brother, Tommy, with wife and kids, as will Brownie, just ashes now, those photos in frames around that small wooden box, pictures of him as a boy, as a baseball player, as a handsome young man.

A person can know everything that will happen, but still never be sure what it means. Going home will be this way—an illusion of solidity—and I'm sure that young Mouse will be waiting for me as well. I know I'll have to go to the pond to look for him and Brownie. I'll need to make that pilgrimage.

I had a dream one time. In it, I'm hiking along some perfect vision of country road. One of those grand-tour type journeys. Rolling pastures and hills, stone houses off in the distance, cows, sheep, haystacks. All of a sudden in the dream I have to stop. I can't seem to go on any farther. Maybe a storm is coming. Maybe I sense some danger down the hill. Whatever the reason, I can see myself huddled along the edge of the ravine. Loose rocks and lovely vistas all around, but I'm bent with great concentration over some kind of work.

In the dream there's nothing ludicrous to this task of mine. There's nothing unreasonable about how serious I am. It's clearly life or death for me, whatever this is. My wife is standing off to the side. I'd not known she was there, yet in the dream I'm not a bit surprised when Betty asks what I am doing. Without so much as glancing up to her—can't spare a moment away from this very important work—I'm telling her that I'm writing to God for forgiveness.

So maybe that's what I'm doing here.

Asking forgiveness.

Even Brownie would scoff this aside. He'd have no patience for this sort of nonsense. He'd come back from the dead to haunt me. My best friend from childhood kills himself, and I'm on my way home to his funeral, trying to dial us back to some magic spot, some moment where things began to go wrong.

We once found a gun in the woods, and never did we tell anyone what happened that afternoon. Maybe it was shame. Maybe it was fear. Maybe it was some test of friendship. Hard to say why, but the gun became a secret we kept to the end. It hovered like a curse, the two of us marooned at the edge of the pond with this thing. But still a person could find himself forever circling back to a place, as if some missing detail would have to reveal itself eventually, as if one afternoon held everything that came later in a life.

I am a ghost sifting for something solid in the ashes.

— 4 —

If only I'd had what it took to shoot him. Not so much killed or crippled Brownie, just taken the gun and put a nice clean wound into his shin or foot, Brownie writhing in pain and blood, and this Mouse character running for all he was worth through the cemetery for help. Now that'd be something they could have told about us down at the Elks. We'd be able to dine out on this sort of story for the rest of our lives. One of those lasting moments—The Day Mouse Shot Brownie—this aria of pure boyhood stupidity, the two of us connected as permanently as brothers in this half-funny, half-horrifying, totally fucked up kind of way.

Older, wiser, we'd tell everyone how I spazzed and put a bullet into his foot. Brownie'd take off his shoe and sock, if the mood was right, let that mangled toe *breathe*! Let that shit see the light of *day*! It'd be a comedy routine of ours, Brownie saying nobody messes with the Mouse, which would be my cue to stand up and be all, "Mouse no more, muthafuckas!"

Imagine the presence of mind it would take to stand calm as cake and squeeze that trigger straight into the top of a sneaker. Kids able to do that would have been able to do anything they wanted in the world. No stopping two little psychos like these. We'd have skated through the rest of life just fine. We'd have stacked a woodpile any way we damn well pleased, no matter how picky someone's father might be. Nothing could have touched us, no one able to piss and moan about how useless we were. We'd have shot a gun before we drank a beer, before we kissed a girl, before we drove a car.

Wish the gun had done some of this work for us. Wish it made us killers. Or turned us back to normal kids. Either way we'd have known who we really were inside. If the gun didn't give us power, if it didn't end up having any consequence in our lives, then at least we could have lumped it in with all the other dumb-shit things we stumbled into as we were growing up. We once set an empty field on fire with a lighter and aerosol can. The fire department came. The flames cleaned out the whole factory yard of old scrub trees and pallets, that acrid taste lingering for weeks. We once drove the Cutlass into a ditch. We once found a pistol in the woods after school. Just another lark among larks. The gun could have been like that time we discovered his father's gin over the kitchen sink, gun like my stomach being pumped at the hospital that afternoon, gun like the job I had of hosing down my pants in the yard the next morning. I'd shit myself. I'd woken with cuts and bruises. I'd gone on some kind of journey.

Wish we'd been able to joke at least once about the gun, put it all in some sort of perspective. Wish we'd been able to see the pistol the way we saw Father Barney with his hernia tests at CYO basketball. Wish the gun were more like the time with the pay phone at the aquarium—one of the countless things to look back on and laugh about when we were older—a school field trip, everyone waiting in line, that briny smell of mollusks and horseshoe crabs in the welcome tanks of the foyer, and then the coin-return slot of the phone we couldn't help but finger as we stood there.

Wish the gun were exactly like this. Wish it were just some bit of mischief. Something we couldn't help but engage. Like the pay phone in front of us, what self-respecting boy could resist? Who would not have had to lift the receiver to his mouth and ear? Who would not feel the need to dial that dirty little zero?

There used to be these things called pay phones on street corners back then. They were housed in glass booths, or they were attached to walls under the awnings of gas stations or convenience stores, or they were sometimes tucked out of the way in foyers, halls, and vestibules of office buildings and restaurants. The fancier booths had wooden seats and smelled of furniture polish. Recessed spotlights glowed to life from the ceiling as you closed the folding privacy doors. For a dime you could make a local call and talk forever. For long distance an operator would come onto the line to help complete the connection, tell you how much it would cost and how long you could talk. If you happened to have no coins, the operator could reach out like a medium in a séance, asking the other party if they were willing to accept the charges. You could hear the faraway voices saying yes or no.

One might have thought things such as operators and phone booths and record albums and clock radios and so much else would have been more permanent. One might have thought that it would never seem necessary to document, if only for historical interest and accuracy, how telephones had this steady drone when you picked up the receiver (a dial tone, they called it), that steady hum letting you know that the line was working, and that the operator (a real, live person) would be there when you dialed zero. There were times you could dip your finger into the coin slot and come up with a jackpot of quarters and dimes. The world could be magic in this way.

Our gun had that same kind of poetry to it. And so did the field trip to the aquarium. One of those open-ended moments that seemed to always come back. A humid warmth, a thick taste of salt, and our whole middle school waiting in line near those welcoming tanks, and then Brownie dialing that zero on the pay phone, him handing the receiver to me, the greasy mouthpiece touching straight to my lips, and the operator (she'd be all nasal and faraway) asking if she can help, and me without a moment's thought blurting out, "Suicide Hotline, please."

Of all possible things to say. It'd be a bolt of lightning, and it'd strike so close I'd jump back and slam the receiver to the cradle. That jangle of coins inside the face of the phone. Everyone laughing.

But what could a kid know? Not like he could see something coming from decades away. Just a coincidence—the air all fishy and hard to breathe—and yet of the thousand things he could have blabbed into the receiver at that moment, why did it have to be this?

Mrs. Jankowski would glare from the front of the line for us to behave, everyone starting through the turnstiles into the aquarium. We'd move slowly forward, but then that big blare of phone in the alcove behind us. It was a loud crazy ringing so sudden and shrill, Brownie lunging back to stop the sound.

"Hello?"

He'd go quiet and pale as he listened, the rest of us stringing ahead toward the turnstiles. Inside the aquarium he'd pull me aside and whisper that the police were on their way.

Always we had to banish the weak and soft in ourselves. That one afternoon at the pond, in order to conquer the gun, we had to squint for any cracks in each other, Brownie moving as if he slept every night of his life with a weapon under his pillow, me standing rubbing my hands together against the cold, the air licking cool off the trees, and our whole world contained in this arena of pines, water shining black, just the two of us, nobody else around, no one having any reason to be here. The trigger moved just slightly under his finger. Not enough to touch any bullets to life. Not enough to make anything happen, though I knew also to be wary, suspicious, as if it'd be just like Brownie to be playing me here, only teasing that he couldn't pull the trigger, only pretending to be shaky and weak, as if any moment he might swoop in with some last-second *gotcha*!

Yet those cords in his neck would have been hard to fake. The barrel of the pistol trembling as he strained, Brownie pointing at the trees. He pulled the hammer, trying to find some lever or toggle. He aimed again higher, up at the sky, trigger cutting into his finger.

This went on for a while, Brownie with the gun like this, until finally he let out this long breath, like steam escaping, his whole body deflating. He lowered his arms, saying it was stuck or jammed or frozen or something.

Wrong of me to feel happy, bad to outwardly gloat, yet how good to have him try as hard as he could and fail. I worked to chew that grin off my face. What a relief when even he couldn't get the pistol to fire.

No bullet, meaning nothing worth remembering, meaning nothing worth keeping as a secret.

He must have seen what I was thinking.

"This is so lame," he said.

I wanted to help him, the two of us looking out at the pond, the gun in Brownie's hand. I tried asking if he was hungry or cold or anything—things I must have been feeling myself—and I tried wondering if maybe the gun got dumped in the woods because it was broken, Brownie saying there had to be some rivet or lock we were missing.

"We can't be this dumb," he said, "can we?"

"Sure we can," I told him.

And Brownie shook his head and said no. He said there had to be some clasp, his fingers pressing every screw and nodule of the gun, like it was a puzzle he couldn't figure out.

I must have been smiling, because Brownie told me to stop and help. He flipped the gun backward in his hand, holding it like a hammer now, his fist tight around the barrel. Then he tapped the edge of the handle on the concrete of the spillway.

He hit lightly at first, such a delicate clink of metal.

I said, "Be careful."

I said, "Not so hard."

I said, "Hold it the other way."

"Yes, Mother," said Brownie—and he raised the gun over his head and chopped down hard at the wall, that loud chock of steel against stone and spillway, and this lighter chuck whiplashing back to us from the other side of the pond—and all I could think was the bullet, if the gun went off now, would go straight into his chest or stomach. You could trace the line clean through him. The only thing possible was to watch and hope and wait for the worst to simply happen.

But nothing ever turned out the way you imagined. In many ways, Brownie would be hitting that wall for the rest of his life. He would be there, hammering the gun until something gave way inside. One moment the gun was as hard as an ax, and the next it clanked loose, a broken sound, like spoons and forks, a sudden gap appearing at the base of the handle, Brownie opening the gun even more. He had that told-you-so grin on his face, him coming over to show the shine of the metal track, which he eased from out of the bottom of the grip.

There were bullets inside, that line of cartridges golden and glossed and clean. He slid the magazine out of the gun—long scrape of sand and oil as he pulled the metal free—and then Brownie handed me the pistol so that he could concentrate, the gun there in my palm, my fingers around it, the outside rough and gritty, the inside pristine and gleaming.

So different without the magazine—the balance off—the pistol gutted and empty, those fresh nicks in the handle, the sharp bites from where Brownie had been hitting. A smell of sewing machine oil from inside.

Brownie touched each of the bullets with his fingertip. One, two—there were six, the row of them fitting one on top of the other—and he slipped the last cartridge from its slot. A spring closed the space so instantly that it seemed not to have happened at all. And maybe this was part of the act, Brownie producing a single bullet, lifting it to the light between his fingers.

He put it to his nose to smell. For a second he might have slipped it into his mouth, but then he stepped over and reached it out to me, pressing the bullet to my hand. I half expected my flesh to go soft, half watched for the metal to push warm as a knife into me.

Brownie took the gun and lined the magazine back inside the handle. I wondered aloud if there could be any bullets anywhere else—some chamber we didn't know about—and Brownie shrugged and said not our problem and pushed the clip home with the heel of his hand. It was something from a television show, Brownie firm and tough, standing there impressive. He lifted his arm and tried again to fire the pistol. He used two hands, and I braced for the sound, like it would be different now.

I dimmed my eyes and hummed for the pistol to go off.

"Gun, go off now," I chanted.

"Gun, go now," I kept saying.

I squeezed the bullet in my fist, trying to will the pistol to fire—and all my pleading inside only seemed to push the hope away, Brownie unable to fire the gun because he and I wanted it to happen so bad.

He finally tossed the pistol to the ground. He was just so done with it, gun thrown away like some piece of trash, this thing lying in the gravel near the wall, sprigs of tall grass leaning over it.

I took a mitten from out of my pocket. I could feel Brownie watching as I picked up the gun and brushed the sand from the handle. I placed the mitten on the wall. I laid the gun meticulous and gentle on top of that small wool hand. I didn't want the metal to be hurt any more than it was, didn't want the gun feeling neglected and cold. It should rest and feel comfortable and safe. It shouldn't worry, I said as I stroked along the grain of its face. I rubbed the smudges from the metal, trying to coax the pistol calm.

Brownie kept watching, and when I turned he shook his head to mock me.

"See?" he said. "That's nice."

"You're just jealous," I told him.

"Even the fact that you have mittens," said Brownie.

I touched the sharp wounds in the handle, as if to apologize to the gun for Brownie, and he clucked his tongue and turned and walked away through the ferns toward the woods and cemetery. I wanted him to keep going. If only he'd disappeared into the trees, that crunch of steps fading to nothing. Inside I was humming for him to keep walking.

"Just keep it moving," I was saying.

"Just go," I was telling him.

I kept pressing the back of his windbreaker with my eyes. I pushed him with my mind, told him not to stop. I got him past where the campfires were in the winters, past the logs and burned rocks where we'd sit to change into our skates. I got him to the next edge of trees, but then he stopped to open his pants, Brownie pissing into the ferns, me saying in my mind for him to leave.

Saying, "Go away."

Saying, "Go back to the cemetery."

Saying, "Leave place already."

In my own little head-case way, I must have known what would be good for Brownie. I must have known exactly what he needed—to be gone from here—yet I also wanted what would be best for me, which was for him to never go anywhere.

Nothing to be proud of, the way I calmly slipped the bullet he gave me into the pocket of my jeans, the way I lifted the pistol from the mitten. It was my turn with the gun.

I pulled the slide and pressed some combination that seemed to catch. Some mechanism clicked in the pistol, the trigger like a clock about to strike, the whole thing letting me know it was ready to shoot. I waited for Brownie to turn.

— 5 —

The gun we found was an M-1911. This was the standard-issue sidearm for the United States military from 1911 to 1986—World War I, World War II, the Korean War, Vietnam—and, as such an integral part of a soldier's life, it only made sense that every essential to this weapon and others would be laid out in great, almost loving detail in the *Basic Field Manual of the United States Armed Forces*.

Prepared under the direction of the Department of War, *The Soldier's Handbook* (as it was also known) had spaces at the front to record a SOLDIER'S NAME, SERIAL NUMBER, RIFLE NUMBER, CHIEF BENEFICIARY (SIX MONTHS' PAY). It had blank pages near the back for LAST WILL AND TESTAMENT. Scattered throughout were common-sense reminders, bits of fatherly advice—*be loyal, be alert, be determined, be a member of the team*. There were chapters on INSIGNIA AND CLOTHING, MILITARY DISCIPLINE, THE MARCH, THE CAMP, THE BIVOUAC, THE PROPER USE OF MAPS, THE SECURITY OF SMALL GROUPS. But the vast bulk of the manual was devoted, by necessity, to *ARMS AND EQUIPMENT*.

Diagrams, instructions, warnings: all of these things were waiting in a strongbox in my childhood room. What I'm trying to say is, I had an old metal footlocker with my father's papers and letters under my bed growing up. I had his cancelled checks, his medical records, his window-washing receipts, pocketknife, car keys, wallet. I had a half-used packet of mint-flavored toothpicks, a certificate for marksmanship from the United States Marine Corps. And I had a copy of his *Basic Field Manual*, those gray and pulpy pages, and this figure of the gun waiting there for me all along:

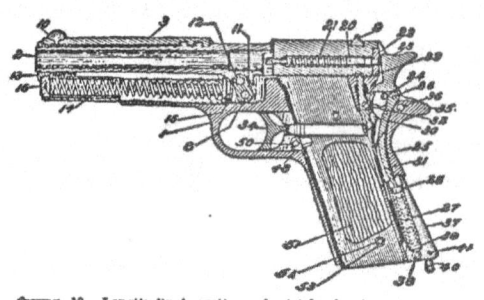

FIGURE 13.—Longitudinal section of pistol, showing component parts in assembled position.

Simple, reliable, the M-1911 weighed just under three pounds unloaded, its magazine holding seven rounds. *CARE OF PISTOL—To prevent wear and tear on the working parts of your pistol, the metal should be cleaned and covered with a thin, uniform coat of oil. • A dirty, dry pistol will have stoppages that may make it useless in battle. • A failure of your pistol in battle may cost you your life.*

• • •

What I'm really trying to say is, I never really knew my father. I met him twice before he died when I was ten. I remember going to the farm with my mother. A cow stepped on my foot that first visit. And there he was—this man I barely even had as an *idea*—my father rummaging an old Indian hatchet from some pile of junk to stop my crying.

Somewhere along the line I had gotten it into my head that the more you used a blade the sharper it would become. With that in mind, I started chopping branches that had fallen from the trees in the yard. I sat on the steps of the porch and unraveled the decorative tassels from the handle. I made quick work of those long strips of leather, chopping them into ant-sized pieces. I wanted this tomahawk to be as sharp as a razor.

This would be what I'd most remember: the man appearing at the screen door, staring down at me to ask what have I got there? And this boy offering up these tiny bits of leather in the cup of his palm. That cringe on my father's face. Him turning without a word.

Our second visit wouldn't go much better. There were beagle puppies out in the barn. I forgot to close the pen, and they all got loose, the puppies chasing after the chickens. My favorite fell between the bales of hay. You could hear her crying deep in some crevice. I ran to get my father from the house. Bale by bale he had to break down nearly the entire hayloft to rescue the dog. An afternoon's work for the man.

My mother and I would not see my father again after this. Pulmonary embolism, living room couch, bowl of melted ice cream on his lap: that was how he died. And in the parking lot of the funeral home that summer, my uncle gave me my father's things. His wallet, his keys, the papers in his room. All in a small metal locker the size of a baby's coffin.

Sometimes, growing up in that room by the cemetery, on nights I couldn't sleep, I would lie in bed so alert to the dark. It would have a viscous quality, a black plushness that made it increasingly difficult to breathe. All the shadows in their right places, everything appearing perfectly natural, yet somehow I'd know I was not alone. From out of this he'd emerge as a creak of floor near the bed, my father inching toward me in the dark. He'd move so quiet and slow in the watery black of the room.

Not a friendly visit. Not there to comfort anyone. He never arrived to give solace or relief. More this empty volume, the man, and then a cold hand on the back of my neck. Not hard, not heavy, but not exactly lifting either. There'd be this strange and steady pressure that I knew to be him, the hair on my arms going electric. I'd get myself nice and riled up. I'd listen for my mother sleeping in the next room, that rolling into shore of her breathing. I'd stare my eyes raw with the traffic light outside my window, the steady throb of red on the gloss of Woodstock Avenue.

Nights like these I'd get up and check my collections: my shells, my acorns, my pebbles and bottle caps, old nails, pull tabs. I'd take books from the shelves or baseball cards from their piles, the piles sorted by team, the teams sorted by player position. I'd dawdle over some project halfway built on the desk—an airplane model, a cardboard gas station—and then that strongbox under the bed would occur to me, as if I'd completely forgotten it existed.

I'd slide it out into the light. I'd open the latch—that stale tang of metal—and this would be my father for me.

Tin and old papers, my fingers leafing through the letters. A street address, numbers scribbled on the back of an envelope, doctor's appointment, smudge of grease—the debris of his life I'd pick over, as if sniffing for specks of meat on a bone.

Loose buttons and coins at the bottom, the wooden matches, and then always those black-and-white photos: my mother and father at the farm (late afternoon, front porch); my father as a young soldier sitting with his parents (handsome young prowl of a man in his uniform, cap pushed back off his face, his mother holding him down with her elbow); this man asleep in a chair with a baby on his chest (me staring out wide awake); and so on.

When I am older, my mother will tell me that she and my father would make love while I was outside playing at the farm. What was a person supposed to do with that sort of knowledge, the two of them in the house together? Or the fact that my father (him with that sweepstakes smile of his) would die, of all days, on my mother's birthday? How were these details supposed to lie still? How was this supposed to fit together?

I never meant to become my mother about such things, but it was hard not to want to find meaning in these objects. I must have learned by heart from her how to select omens. Tiny seeds to encourage. No such things as accidents. Everything having a purpose.

The *Basic Field Manual of the United States Armed Forces* was waiting there in my room on the day we found the gun. It was lying under my bed all along. But it was much too subtle, much too quiet, much too vague to be of any use at the time. I'd find it years too late, well beyond any help it might have been for me and Brownie.

Still, I would always want it to be my father who was arranging these objects as messages for me. Every time I opened that old metal box of leftover junk, there'd be something new, some detail I had never quite noticed before. A new postmark, a fresh pack of chewing gum, a fresh dollar bill in his wallet.

I'd know this wasn't truly possible, but then that feathery brush of fear in my room at night. I could feel his presence hovering by the door. He would be there in the room. No one could ever convince me otherwise. No one could ever lift this away from me.

How could I *not* wish to find meaning in a neatly folded certificate for marksmanship from the United States Marine Corps? Wasn't I born for this kind of work? Was I not meant to hold this Mercury dime, this window-cleaning receipt? Didn't the mere survival of a thing make it somehow significant? Didn't the simple fact of an object, its persistence, stand for something important? And was there any chance I could ever open that *Basic Field Manual* and not feel my father trying to direct me? How could I not want to hear the man's voice in that metal box, my father trying to tell me something through these leavings?

Do not leave a loaded weapon where someone else may unknowingly pick it up. • Keep the safety lock on at all times, particularly when advancing, as you may catch your trigger in brush and kill yourself or your comrade. • Never point a weapon at anyone unless you intend to kill him. • Do not assume that you or your companions are safe.

—6—

Brownie would never quite go away. There at the pond he'd be out in the ferns zipping his pants. I'd be standing at the spillway with the gun aimed at him. He'd start back through the vines and brush. He'd kick at the blackened stones, the charred scraps of the old fire pit, Brownie not looking up at me. I had to make pig grunts for him to notice, Brownie waving me off, as if even with a gun I was nothing to worry about.

Just a nuisance, just a pest, I held the gun at him and said, "It wants to shoot you."

He didn't seem fazed in the least, and I saw that smear of a grin on his face, Brownie standing in front of me just so incredulous.

"The gun wants to?" he asked.

"Yes," I said.

"Bullets say anything?" he asked.

I nodded the barrel up and down.

I put the gun to my ear to listen.

I said, "They're saying, 'Shoot Brownie.'"

Such trials I put him through, such patience he had, the soft of my finger on the trigger. I moved the gun closer to his chest. A small reach and I could have poked him, Brownie saying, "There's something wrong with you."

"I realize that," I said.

I poked him with the muzzle of the gun, telling him it wasn't locked anymore.

"How d'you know?" he asked.

I put the pistol to my ear, and Brownie was like, "It told you."

"It trusts me," I said.

"Good for you," said Brownie.

He walked toward the spillway in disgust, looking down at the rocks below, the stream leading off into the woods. The moment had passed, obviously, and I pointed the gun away toward the pond and trees. I raised the sight to the sky, two hands on the pistol, and I slowly closed my finger on the trigger. It went smooth. Four pounds of pressure all the way down, textbook action to it, clean steady press along the loop of guard.

Nothing stopping the slide.

Bracing for it—that big clap of the shot—gun kicking loud and abrupt in my hands. Arms jumping away, that hard bite at the webs of thumbs, my ears with a siren inside, a ringing and chewing pressure, a taste of metal in the air.

I could feel him staring at me—Brownie all big eyed and amazed—and I lowered my arms and worked hard not to turn to him. I didn't want to see him smiling. I didn't want my own feelings overpowered by whatever he was going to say. I wanted to figure out what I felt. I wanted to catch it before it was gone. I stared at the trees, clouds hanging like a tarp over everything.

A dog barked in the distance, a ripple swam across the pond, and the bullet must have still been flying, this sizzle of hornet biting down somewhere miles away, this tiny pinpoint of evil arriving out of the blue, finding its way to some mailman on a sidewalk, some windshield of a car, or some innocent dog in a yard.

My face hot with fear, I turned to Brownie, him smiling at me.

"You suck," he said.

"What?"

"I want to shoot something."

He glanced to the gun at my side and bent to pick the tiny brass casing from the dirt. I asked if it was hot, and he rolled it between his fingers, bringing it to his face to smell, and then he simply flipped the thing away into the pond like a coin.

He must have known I'd want it, yet there was Brownie, plopping that brass shell into the water.

I took half a step, as if to go in, but then I reminded myself that I was the one who had just fired the gun. It was mine, the pistol in my hand. It was solid. I was strong. I could feel the faint ticking of a tiny clock inside. I could touch that bullet in my pocket, and Brownie would have nothing, though already he was kicking through the ferns and grasses, scouting for something he could shoot. A beer bottle would have been perfect. A soda can, a frog, anything.

Nothing but the two of us at this edge of pond. Among the many things that would stand out in my mind from all of this, one of the strangest was how, up to a certain point, we seemed so thoroughly alone that day. No allies, no help.

Everywhere we turned that afternoon with the gun went bleak and empty, Brownie saying, "Not even a bird."

Me saying, "It's like they cleaned the woods."

"I know," he said, "it's weird."

"Really weird," I told him.

We fanned out—a sort of boat launch, the shore sandy and shallow before us—and we said there had to be fish to shoot. There had to be turtles, we said. There had to be ducks or snakes or something.

Later, we'd name all the things that were hiding from us in the pond that day. Our eighth-grade science project: *THINGS FOUND IN A POND,* by Steven M. Brownell and William J. Lychack. Such penmanship we'd have, such signatures, such teamwork, such unconscious forces at work in the lives of boys. We'd relive the pond as much as possible. We'd compensate for this one afternoon, the two of us setting out to find whatever we must have missed that day. We'd paste pictures of salamanders, crayfish, beavers, leeches, newts. We'd go to the town hall and trace a topographical map of the land surrounding the pond. We'd color in the streams and brooks of the watershed. We'd make roads and culverts, all the evidence of civilization, the foundation of an abandoned barn, an old well, stone walls, houses.

We'd be good students, eager for praise, our whole lives desperate to prove we weren't spoiled and lazy and half-assed. Even his mother, so tough to please, would have had to admire how faithfully we reported the contents of a pond. Great blue herons, mallard ducks, snails, cattails, lilies, dragonflies. We'd diagram the life cycle of frogs—that whole arc of egg to tadpole, froglet to full-fledged frog to eggs all over again. We'd make a display of fish common to a pond such as ours. Perch, trout, bass, pickerel. There'd be the endless varieties of sunfish: bluegill, pumpkinseed, spotted bass, largemouth bass, smallmouth bass, rock bass, warmouth, crappies...

In the real world, at the real pond, we couldn't tell one species of sunfish from another. They were all just kivvers to us—tough little hungry fish that would pick your bait clean like nobody's business. You'd think we might have identified with them more—those cunning little thieves, sharp edged and needy—but the kivvers only seemed to bring out the cruel in us. They were unlucky to be caught, and we punished them by swinging and slapping their bodies against the ground until the hook tore through their lip or cheek. Sometimes their stomachs would be pulled out though their mouths, and we'd laugh.

Where did the meanness come from?

When did we stop letting ourselves feel for things?

I don't remember ever once bothering to kick one back into the pond, poor fish panting in the dirt, blood in its gills. When did that shrug of indifference start with us?

There at the pond, brushing through the grasses and ferns for something to shoot, Brownie started saying we should go home now.

I said we should keep looking. I kept saying we'd find something, kept saying he could shoot at anything, but he shook his head no and started toward the cemetery. To stop him, I asked why he was being so weird about the gun.

He turned and said, "I don't know."

"Just shoot at nothing," I told him.

"I can't," said Brownie.

He said he had to shoot at a real thing. He moved past the campfire, and I followed with the gun. It seemed hopeless, but then this glimpse: an old oil drum in the vines and creepers. They used it for fires on the ice, thing all blackened and rusted and hiding behind the trees and brush.

I hollered for him.

I went giddy, and he saw what I was pointing to and came back. We had the oil barrel to shoot, and I hurried the gun to him, the two of us wading through the ferns, the oil barrel cowering in the scrub brush, thing all bent and full of holes, completely at our mercy.

Brownie put the gun execution-style to its head.

He held it there and waited.

"Any last words?" I asked the barrel.

"Go ahead, Brownie, put it out of its misery," I said.

He stood there, and slowly his arm wilted, the gun hanging down and away from the oil drum. He looked over to me, and I had a sinking sense that he could shoot me now. It was there in his eyes, the pause, the hesitation, Brownie saying, "I think it has to be moving."

I stared at him.

"Is that dumb?" he asked.

"No," I told him.

"It can't just be sitting there," he said.

I said, "I'll roll it for you."

And I cut through the prickers toward him and pulled weeds and roots off the oil barrel, Brownie just standing there as I rocked the thing out of the brush. I was a witness to his weakness—just a glance and I could see him not knowing what was happening here—and I kicked the barrel forward over the ferns, a swath pressing flat and bright behind me.

I needed to get him back to being Brownie.

I needed him to shoot the gun.

I straightened the drum and got it rolling back the other way, the ferns like cut grass to smell, Brownie slouching and tired with the gun at the end of his arm.

I tried to toughen him back to life, calling him names, saying that even I had shot the gun.

I watched as he slowly put the pistol in his pocket, the heavy shape of it hanging in his jacket. He turned and the two of us set off into the sunset, away from the pond. We made our way, me and Brownie walking back to the cemetery, back over the graves, back through the gates.

In those days, in the kind of town where we lived, a pair of boys were supposed to get into at least a little trouble. As long as they looked out for each other—didn't let their friends drown in the river or get run over by a train—it was the job of us kids to push the outskirts of what was allowed.

What else were fathers supposed to drink about down at the Elks? Nobody wanted boys too goody-goody. Even mothers like mine would get on the phone if they had something juicy to tell their girlfriends. Nothing could be that bad, just as long as we were home safe for dinner, that horn on top of the fire station calling us back every evening, six o'clock sharp.

But it was still early, still plenty of time between here and home, the fire station nowhere close to signaling. We had hours left to go. We passed the church, the supermarket, the package store. Cars swam past as we went to Brownie's through town. We moved along the sidewalks and shortcuts, all these boring streets of ours, all the people hiding behind their curtains, friends from school safe in their houses, Brownie with the gun in his pocket. We passed the gas station, the old mills, that fresh-paint smell near the river, clean as bleach, that familiar menthol burn clearing the nostrils.

We started telling each other how everyone who stayed away was just so incredibly lucky. Even the birds and squirrels were happy to go missing. It got to where we said we wanted no one to get so much as a glimpse of us on our way home. It was like we were trying to escape, me and Brownie willing everybody gone from our sight. We were a pair of boys wishing to slip by quick and unscathed.

But then how many front yards and driveways before the inevitable had to happen? How far did we think we could get without running into anyone? How long before a fear turns into a secret kind of wish?

—PART TWO—

— I —

One night we left a shard of glass in a drink for his father. Such rage we must have felt. This was after college, after a lot of things. We were in and out of each other's lives, but every so often Brownie and I would bartend together. Usually some catering gig at the Lions Club. One of those birthday-slash-retirement parties, and the broken glass was entirely my fault. I'd been told to use the metal scoop. I'd been told not to be lazy, but still I dipped straight into the ice with the glass, that quick slice waking me, the blood like heat from my fingertips. Brownie couldn't stand the sight of it, and he winced and looked away and called me a fricken idiot.

He got a towel for me and took what was left of the highball glass. It was jagged and half-missing. He set it to the side of the metal sink. The cloth soaked through with blood almost immediately. Such a deep and heavy red. Remarkable how fast and warm.

Brownie pulled a fresh apron from the cabinet for me to use.

The cut was a long clean line across my first knuckle—would always have the scar on my hand as proof—and I pinched it hard to stop the bleeding, the burn so clear it felt almost pleasant. Brownie poked around the well bottles for pieces of glass. He started the hot water running in the sink and told anyone who came up that we were out of mixed drinks. Beer and wine only.

He took care of things from there. He could do this job alone, probably easier for him without me. He poured pitchers of hot water into the ice bin. I stood off to the side and could feel my heart in the cut, each beat a bloom in the hand. There were steam clouds coming off the ice, and someone was giving a toast at the other end of the hall, and then Brownie's father arrived to the bar.

Mr. Brownell lined these jobs up for us, and not for a single minute did he let anybody forget it. He once got Brownie set up at the power company—real bread-and-butter spot in the union—but that wonderful son of his stopped showing up for work. Brownie did the same with college, not going to classes, then taking a semester off, then not quite getting back to it. He did the same with the jobs at the lumberyard and the daycare center, and he did the same with Liz and Maureen, Brownie not so much disappearing as simply not appearing anymore.

He was, by nature, unable to do anything that his father wanted him to do. Even if he knew his father was right, even if he knew his father was only trying to help, Brownie still had to make his own way, deny whatever the man offered.

It remained a real question right to the end: did he do everything only to spite his father?

• • •

If Mr. Brownell came to the bar and wanted a Seven-and-Seven, then it only followed that Brownie would have to resist the man's wish somehow. That is to say, his father wouldn't have thought twice about coming behind the bar and helping himself to the last dregs of ice, giving himself a good long pour of Seagram's, a splash of soda.

We'd stand back and let him do all this. It'd not be out of the ordinary to watch his father stir the drink with his finger. That tinsel of ice in the glass. So gratifying, so anxious, me and Brownie standing there, the drink in Mr. Brownell's hand, man asking if we were having a good night.

We must have said yes or sure or whatever, though all that mattered was that first dainty sip. We were ready to run for the exit, ready also to stand up and fight. Hard to tell which would be better, me and Brownie tense for whatever came next, my finger with each pulse right there in the knuckle.

Brownie's father put a twenty on the bar and took the next sip, chewing a piece of ice, the man eyeing us the whole time, saying there was something funny going on. He said we were probably on drugs or something.

We weren't on drugs, said Brownie.

The man tipped the rest of his drink back in one swallow and pushed the tall glass across to Brownie, who took the glass and scooped what was left of the ice. Brownie gave a nice long count of Seagram's, quick gun of 7-Up, fresh napkin on the bar.

His father with that pinky dipping again, as if he was not at all impressed, as if Brownie was always such a disappointment to him. The man could go from right to righteous in the space of a drink, and he called us lightweights and had a sip, napkin clinging to the bottom of the glass.

Brownie took the money and wiped the bar with a rag. He helped himself to a beer from the fridge, one for him, one for me. Brownie's father said cheers.

There must have been people coming over to the bar. There must have been a game on the television. There must have been a whole world streaming around this little scene of ours. American flags hanging from the ceiling, cigarette machine by the bathroom door, plaques and awards, a phone on the wall, though all I remember was how we stood waiting for his father to take that one last gulp, the man saying that we were made out of butter.

He had a way of speaking that left you curious. And then they had a way of talking, as well, Brownie and his father with these quick jabs back and forth, as if just slap-boxing with each other, as if it was nothing personal, as if it might have even been affection. None of this would make sense to me—the hatred and love flush up against each other like that—but then what would I know about anything? Especially about fathers and sons?

I watched. I studied. I took notes, Mr. Brownell with another sip of his drink, Brownie asking his father, "What's that mean—to be made out of butter?"

"Well, let's see," said the man, "if you're made out of butter, it means that no matter what you become, you're still only going to be butter in the end. You can become the best sculpture in the world, but you're still only butter."

"I like butter," said Brownie. "It makes things taste better."

He reached over and clinked my bottle.

We drank to that.

"I love to put butter on my toast," Brownie told him.

"Be a smart ass," said the man. "Let's watch how far that gets you. Working out pretty well up to now, wouldn't you say?"

Still that glass in his hand, and Brownie's father raised it to us and said salute. He finished his drink. He stopped, pursed his lips, and then slowly swallowed. The rest of his body held perfectly still as he set down his empty drink and pulled a long fang of glass from out of his mouth.

We were shocked at ourselves—one swallow away from his heart, our capacity for evil, that resentment we must have had simmering inside—but Brownie's father didn't seem surprised in the least. He seemed to know that our anger was misplaced. He seemed to appreciate whenever we showed signs of life. If nothing else, it demonstrated some initiative on our part, the man holding the piece of glass up to the light.

"Guys," he said, "you might want to check that ice of yours. Seems a *little* off tonight."

— 2 —

My heart went down even before we saw him, Crawford standing on the steps of the apartment building where he lived, Brownie saying to me, "Hey, look, there's Crawf!"

He'd not seen us yet—on the street, on our way skulking home—and I pulled Brownie back, held his arm, his hands deep in his pockets.

"Don't worry," said Brownie. "We'll be nice."

"Let's just leave," I said.

We were halfway across to him—Crawford still only a kid in front of his house, unaware of anything bad approaching, our friend so innocent out there—but then he saw us and called from the front steps. He was in our class at school and looked as happy and young as a puppy as he waved us over, like we were long-lost buddies.

He seemed so glad to see us that I almost broke into tears. I didn't want Crawford to have any part of this, didn't want him to know anything about the gun, didn't want to share Brownie with him here, didn't want to see what would happen next. I had that warm flood of saliva in my mouth to keep down, Brownie ahead of me, my stomach in my throat.

As usual, I had to work to be smarter than my feelings. I had to swallow whatever urges I had. Crawford with those brave white teeth as he smiled. The stairway, the apartment house, even the sky, everything such a heart breaking gray, just concrete and cinderblock. And Crawford there in the midst of it, much too eager to be friends with us. It made him an easy target—real child's play—and even this close we should have turned and left him safe and untouched. We should have walked off in the other direction, hurt him in a way that Crawford could be grateful for later.

I held Brownie back and said not to do this.

And instead of leaving them there, instead of doing what I knew was the right thing, I continued with Brownie across the street. We slowed as we approached, Crawford at the railing of the steps, his smile going soft as it hung there.

"Hey, Breeze," called Brownie, his voice all big and salesman. "Where've you been?"

I forget why we called him Breeze, except it seemed that nobody was allowed to have only one name in this place. It was a law of nature: all things had to have more than one identity, more than one truth. We called him Crawf, Crawdad, Bimini, Breeze. I'm sure I'm forgetting some, but more important was the way that Brownie spoke, him saying, "We've been looking for you."

We were on the sidewalk with him now, Crawford gripping the rail, not quite believing Brownie, Brownie giving me this look, like was I getting this? Was I in on the joke?

"Tell him, Mouse," said Brownie.

I said we'd been looking for him, and still Crawford stayed on the steps and held the railing as if it were the side of a pool. He was a sweet boy, earnest and simple, and he watched whenever a car passed, his ear a tiny teacup, his cheeks deep brown, skin smooth and perfect. He explained that he'd been here, that he came home normal, like he did every day from school, Brownie cutting him short, saying we were heading back to his house, asking did he want to come along?

It was a charade—a performance we were putting on—and it was there to build a false kind of suspense. The truth was we would be marching any minute to Brownie's house together. The fact was Crawford would want to join us no matter where we were going. Just part of the act, the way we had to pretend to convince Crawford, the way he had to pretend to be convinced, Brownie saying we needed his help to do something, Crawford asking what it was.

"We'll tell you later," said Brownie.

And when I glanced at him, Brownie smiled and flashed the gun to me. It was quick and dark from his pocket. He had that devilish look. It seemed to me that we were two different kinds of bad: Brownie starting as a good person who had to be made to be bad, whereas I seemed bad from the beginning, a bad person who had to choose to be good. I had to guard against myself always. This was what made me the nervous little Mouse, the subservient one, the one full of fear and caution.

Crawford dug for the watch under his cuff, his hands flustered with us leaning over him, Brownie whistling through his teeth, like he was tired of waiting.

In my mind, I saw how we could make it look as if Crawford had done it to himself, his body left out in the scrap fields behind the mills for someone to find, the aviator watch from his father still there loose and big on his wrist, so that it didn't appear to be a robbery, clean sneakers on his feet.

Some kind of violence needed to be released from inside of us boys, something I'd always wish I knew the reason for, something I'd want to understand and let loose somehow, this rising force I'd have to clench my teeth against.

It was four o'clock, he told us.

"Who cares, Breeze," said Brownie. "Are you in or not already?"

Crawford stood as if paused, just waiting with his mouth open.

I asked him if his mother was home.

He said no.

"Will she worry," I asked, "if you're not here?"

"I told her I'd be home," said Crawford.

"Blah, blah," said Brownie. "C'mon, ladies, let's get moving."

Brownie stepped off the curb, as if we'd follow automatically, me and Crawford glancing to each other. I motioned for him to go upstairs to his apartment. I gave him a look that was supposed to make it clear: I knew the confusion he felt; I had the same exact feeling; we should stay right here together.

Brownie turned to ask if we were coming or not.

"Seriously," said Brownie, "you have anything better to do?"

"I shouldn't go," said Crawford, voice more firm.

"Your choice, Breeze," said Brownie—and as easy as that Brownie turned and said adios, amigo.

In a moment we were on our way (or so I hoped), the two of us across the street as Brownie stopped and said to wait. He asked, "Should we show him what we found?"

Brownie told me to get the bullet he'd given me. He had that mean streak turned on me now, those same unbudging eyes, and I worked to get the bullet from my pocket. I carried the cartridge to the step, Crawford still there as before, the bullet warm and solid on my palm.

"There," I said, my hand open, "now you've seen it."

He saw the bullet and looked to me and Brownie.

"Okay," said Crawford.

"It's a bullet," said Brownie.

"Okay," said Crawford.

"Here," I said, trying to give it to him.

"We found it," said Brownie.

"Okay," said Crawford again, taking the bullet in his hand.

How unimpressed he was. His eyes, his attitude, that nonchalance, Crawford looking at the bullet, this thing meaning less than a penny to him, just a dead slug of metal, dull and insignificant in every way. It was only me and Brownie who were under its influence.

In other words, you could reach down into your throat and pull your heart out raw and warm and still beating to show the world, but the world would probably just shrug like it was nothing. The world had its own problems. The world didn't want your heart. It had more than enough hearts already.

I should have known he wouldn't care enough, Crawford giving the bullet back to me. I alone could cherish this object. I alone would keep it pressed in my fist, promising that if one day I should put an end to myself, it would be this bullet that I'd put into my mouth. I carried it in the palm of my hand like a dead wasp and turned to Brownie and said, "Let's go."

Again we were moving, Brownie and me heading down the street together, only it was me who was a step ahead along the sidewalk. It was me walking quickly, leading us to Brownie's house.

I kept walking.

And because I wanted so badly for Crawford to stay away, because there were so many things that would have to go better without him, it only seemed natural that we'd hear his voice calling for us, feel Crawford jogging along from behind.

— 3 —

Maybe they called him Breeze because he ran fast. He played outfield in Little League, so he must have been quick enough to get a good jump on the ball. Maybe his name was something as simple as that. Maybe he did well on some quiz in school, some teacher saying math sure was a breeze for him. Maybe it was something you had to be there for, like Kevin Lavallee becoming Buzza—a can of soda, a bee stinging his lip, and thus a Buzza was born. Maybe Breeze had some kind of story like that. Maybe there was some meaning that he wanted to keep private. Maybe his father called him Breeze as a pet name. Maybe he wanted to hold on to that connection, his father in California, the occasional phone call, the man sending sneakers and jeans from time to time.

Whatever the truth, there seemed an edge to the name, a slight pause, as if there might be something more. Crawford would ask us not to call him that name, which only turned him more and more into Breeze. Somehow the name must have bothered or troubled me. It must have made me wonder enough to look up the word later, to see if there were any hidden meanings.

BREEZE: *n*, (a) light, gentle wind (from four to thirty miles an hour); (b) something easily done; a CINCH; *v*, to move swiftly, quickly, confidently; airily <*He breezed to victory*>; *n* (c) dark residue from the making of charcoal.

BIMINI: the closest Bahamian island to mainland United States, located 80 kilometers (50 miles) east of Miami.

CRAYFISH, CRAWDADS, MOUNTAIN LOBSTERS, MUDBUGS, YABBIES.

"Fricken Breeze," said Brownie, his voice loud enough for Crawford to hear. He knew Crawford would be following, and when he caught up to us Brownie clapped him on the back a little too hard. "Long time, no see, Crawf."

"I'm joining you guys," said Crawford.

"We had a feeling," I said.

Brownie and I moved so that he could take his place between us, Brownie giving me this nod behind Crawford's back, like we were on top of things now. We were part of a mission here. Side by side along the sidewalk, Brownie scuffing along the edge of the grass, hands plunged deep in his pockets, gun there if you knew where to look, me keeping Crawford in the middle.

So vivid could I envision the gun going off that it seemed a thing already accomplished, Brownie's finger with nowhere else to go but the trigger. It was as though we'd been here before, Crawford skipping beside us without a clue, asking what we were thinking of doing at Brownie's. I stepped off the curb to the gutter and kicked along as I had a thousand other times. We crossed from Providence to Church Street, Brownie singing and talking like any other afternoon.

And a person seeing us would have thought what?

That there went the most typical kids in the world—these middle school boys heading home—some kind of soft-focus ad for small-town friendship, the three of them stepping out of *Happy Days* or *Little House on the Prairie*. They were the orphans in *The Boxcar Children*. They were one of those pages from *Life Magazine*, black-and-white photo, kids pretending to be soldiers.

It wasn't far to Brownie's house from here. Less than a mile, and we went along singing snippets of The Cars, The Police, The Who. We sang Cheap Trick. We sang like we were driving with the windows down, the radio loud, the three of us singing Earth, Wind, and Fire. We kicked a flattened soda can. We sang *sad eyes, turn the other way, I don't want to see you cry...*

We cross-country skied along the sand and salt that collected in the gutter from winter, the three of us singing *la la la la Lola...*

We didn't want to ever arrive at Brownie's house.

We dawdled.

We straggled.

We tried to run out the clock, Brownie asking who in our grade would we want to have babies with. Our new word was *fornicate*, none of us quite sure how it worked, the definition in the dictionary only deepening the mystery.

Crawford said he didn't need any babies, saying he was all set for offspring, but Brownie kept pressing, saying we had to want someone. He made a scoreboard out of it, announcing how he'd lead off with a half dozen with

Maureen Rodgers. Brownie suggested Ginny Markowitz, asking who would not want to make a family with her?

Pretty, smart, nice: impossible to disagree with him on Ginny, and I felt that carbonation of nerves in my throat when it was my turn to suggest someone like Michelle, Brownie and Crawford teasing how I waited in the hall for her. Nothing escaped them, me saying it was no big deal, Brownie saying then he would start a little family with her, if I didn't mind so much. I'd go along, playing like it was fine with me. Anything else would have only made it worse.

There was, as we walked, a kind of joy in this. Don't forget that. Don't overlook the happiness. Don't forget we were full of good times. Not everything was heavy. We could be silly and stupid with the best of them. We could be so normal it hurt. To see us on the street would have been to barely notice anything special, cars going by without even a second glance, yet each house we passed felt to us like some last chance to grab the shore. We were getting carried beyond where anyone could save us, streets rivering us away toward Brownie's.

Our town had been home to Gertrude Warner, author of *The Boxcar Children*. She'd lived on Ring Street, across from the dentist's office, a short walk from the old elementary school. She'd been a teacher for many years, writing her mysteries about those orphans who lived in an old train car in the woods. She retired from teaching the year we arrived, but she must have missed kids—frail old bird of a woman—because she'd often visit our class to read her latest story to us. We were supposed to let her know if anything didn't seem right. We were supposed to tell her what we thought from a kid's point of view. We were supposed to say what we remembered most. We were supposed to tell what we thought her stories were about.

More than anything they were about a place and a time. They were about these kids trying to grow up and take care of each other. The town in her books was called Greenfield, though it was really Cargill Falls. We were right there in the pages: Bugbee's Department Store, Trudeau's Hardware, the Button Corp, the textile mills, the old Town Hall, the bridge overlooking the falls, that postcard view from which our town got its name.

And one of us in the class must have asked how she came up with those kids in the boxcar, because I remember her saying how she decided to give up writing. Nothing about it seemed to be working for her. As a final goodbye, she set out to write one final story, something to suit only herself. She had always wanted to live in a freight car as a child. She dreamed of cooking her stew on a woodfire in the old train yards at the edge of town.

We hated having her visit. We groaned at the idea of her boxcar orphans who never seemed to grow up or move away. We suffered for hours, our backs straight, hands folded on top of our desks, feet flat on the floor, that warble voice of hers sending chills, Ms. Warner reading:

> *Even a hammer makes a good pillow if one is tired enough, and the freight car family slept until the nine o'clock church bells began to ring faintly in the valley...*

She could have easily found room in one of her mysteries for kids like us, no need to make up a single thing, that same shake in her throat:

> *The boys meandered their way to Brownie's house, dawdled along, never wanting to arrive. Now that they had Crawford, they found things galore to shoot. Everywhere they looked were empty cans and cats on porches, birds in trees, squirrels on power lines, a young mother taking bags of groceries from her car, a brown rabbit in a yard...*

All verbatim true. Even the rabbit as we got to Addison Street. I really did scurry across to chase the thing into the bushes, Crawford and Brownie all hunky-dory on their side of the street, and me going along on my side, empty gray of asphalt like a stream between us.

We walked parallel to each other until the sidewalks petered out near Brownie's street. It was fancier out here, big green lawns and blacktop driveways, houses standing back all proper and reserved, the three of us merging at the crest toward Brownie's house. Before we saw the roofline, Brownie was already asking us to be quiet. He didn't want the dog to hear our voices. She'd been cooped up, and he didn't want her to have an accident before he could get the key and let her out.

Brownie crossed toward the grass to the side of the house, where they kept a key hooked to the gas meter.

He would be gone for a moment, and Crawford and I would stand on the front walk. There'd be that trade of glances, the two of us stuck there, a slight twitch in my cheek, the corner of my eye starting to flicker.

Crawford saw and looked back toward the street.

I think he felt sympathy for me, which only made things worse.

I had no sympathy for anyone or anything. I started up the front steps of the house and opened the storm door like I owned the place, the long pneumatic pull, the front door painted bright red. I tapped at the wood and looked back to Crawford on the walk, looked to see if Brownie was coming. I tried the handle, the door locked, the dog with those loud sniffs at the bottom gap, and me sing-song whispering to her, asking what was she doing in there all alone?

"And why isn't she out here playing?" I asked.

"And why isn't she saying hello?" I asked

She barked and started digging at the back of the door.

Brownie was halfway across the yard, a good twenty feet to go, and I hit the door with the heel of my fist, the dog in the house with her nails scratching rapid-fire, her barks sharp and loud. If only I had more time, I could have really gotten to Brownie. He had the key on the chain in his hand. He walked normal on the grass, unfazed once again, Brownie unaffected by whatever it was I thought I was doing.

On the steps he said, "You can always go home if you want."

There was not a single snag in his voice. Instead of bringing him down a notch, Brownie rose all the more above me and my jumble of emotions. Not haughty, not triumphant, just years ahead of me again, Brownie calm and commanding over everything.

He unlocked the door.

"Really," said Brownie, "Crawf and I can manage just fine without you."

— 4 —

She was, if I may say, *the perfect dog*. All brindle and ginger leaping off the steps and into the yard, every cliché of happiness right there in flesh and fur, this great burst of dog running around on the lawn, metal tags jangling like coins at her neck. Something clever and nose-driven in her (Jack Russell or Terrier), something sleek and skittish (Whippet or Boxer).

The crooked ears, the lolling tail, she was the dog of our hearts. Couldn't take your eyes off her, the way she ran so wild and happy.

Crawford and Brownie were out on the grass with her now, me standing with my back to the storm door, Brownie scrubbing the dog's washboard of ribs when she got close, him revving her up, saying, "Who's that crazy dog?"

She hadn't been Brownie's for long—not much over a year—and we'd taught her to say hello (one bark). We'd taught her to say give me food (three barks), go Red Sox (three barks), eat me raw (three barks). She'd learned to sit and stay. She knew how to crawl commando-style across the ground on her belly. As Mrs. Brownell would put it, if only we boys could learn half as well as the dog.

We had never given Barkley any reason not to trust us, yet she always flinched if someone lifted a hand too quick near her face. She must have learned this from somewhere. They must have kicked dogs out of the way where she came from. They must have had their reasons, needed dogs to be dogs, whereas we wanted to make this animal one of us.

The Brownells had gotten her last spring, Tommy and Steven riding in the truck with their father on some errand after hockey, the three of them out by the state line on one of those gravel roads, Brownie describing how she looked like an old carpet dumped off to the side when they first saw her. Closer, she looked like a deer lying twisted against the fencing. Someone had tied her there. She stood pressed tight against the wire, mouth wrapped with electric tape.

Mr. Brownell would set the brake on the truck and shut off the engine, telling the boys to stay put. He'd get out of the cab and walk around the front hood, Brownie cranking the window down the rest of the way, Tommy leaning against his brother to see their father stepping through the brush, morning air crisp.

She'd be on the far side of the runoff ditch, unable to turn her head to see the man approaching, the dog going as small as possible, ears down, tail between legs. She'd cringe and wait, nowhere to go, the dog seemingly ashamed of herself, embarrassed by how filthy, by how full of cuts and bugs she was.

In my dream of them, I'd give the boys at least one perfect moment with their father. No lessons to impart, no hidden tests, only the advent of the dog. They would hear their father talking gentle to the dog. They'd watch the man peel the tape from her mouth. He'd cut her free with a pocket knife, her hind legs unsteady and shivering so that she could barely stand, their father's voice soft and high, the man saying, "Easy, girl."

Saying, "No one's going to hurt you."

The dog would lick his hand, and the boys could hold back for only so long, their father leading her around to the truck, Brownie and Tommy out to meet them on the road. They'd see every rib, every lump and hollow. They'd see rope burns, grooves in her neck. They'd get water bottles from their hockey bags, dog drinking from cupped palms. They could smell her skin and fur all caked and stiff, the callouses on her elbows raw.

Their father would boost her up into the bed of the truck and then start them slowly home, mindful of this dog trying to stand in the back, the road corrugated, dust blooming up behind. The brothers had one another to help understand things. They would study the side of their father's face as he drove. They might have talked and carried on in ways I'd not be able to imagine. (My own childhood so invincibly silent compared to theirs.) Maybe they felt suspense riding home with the dog, but probably they already knew she'd be theirs.

As a boy, would it have even crossed Brownie's mind that he shouldn't have everything? Brother, father, house, cottage, and now a dog?

But that was another story.

In the story I wanted to tell for them, they would be making a game plan as they rode home together, their father coaching them on strategy, what to say when they got to their mother. They'd coast into the driveway, get out of the truck, go easy on the doors, the three of them tip toeing with the dog into the garage, that cool of concrete, the smell of oil and gasoline, and their mother waiting there for them. She'd have her arms folded, the woman shaking her head no, saying, "Over my dead body."

Or saying, "Dream on, boys."

Or something to that effect.

Whatever she said would go down in history for them. It would be theirs to remember and laugh about later, how she'd been this anvil in their way, Tommy and Brownie swearing to take care of the dog, the brothers promising to walk her every day, to clean up after her in the yard, their father suggesting they put it in writing, as if that would make a difference.

Mrs. Brownell would remain unmoved by anything they said, and Mr. Brownell would reach to smudge the black from the dog's nose, the creature shying away from his hand.

"It's all right, girl," the man would say, his voice so tender they'd stare as he stroked the dog's face. Did he ever speak to any of them with such gentleness?

No wonder the dog would seem like so much more than a dog. No wonder they thought of her as lucky, the boys tentatively happy as their mother took a deep breath. The dog gave a kind of glimpse into a possible family, like a missing piece they'd found, Mrs. Brownell standing with her hands on her hips, saying, "I'm going to regret this, aren't I?"

—5—

Among the many things that must have come and gone in the mind of a boy that day, there had to have been the very real hope that our gun would simply disappear. The dog loose on the lawn, Brownie returning the key to the gas meter, Crawford standing in the driveway, me stranded on the steps, and couldn't the pistol simply be lost in the shuffle somewhere? It had come into our lives out of the blue, so why couldn't it fall away just as easily?

Brownie came back and got the leash from the house and asked me to take care of the dog. He pressed the leather strap to my arm and said to get her to do her business. I didn't move from where I was, just let the leash fall to my feet, Brownie holding the door for Crawford, saying to him, "Onward, Breeze."

On the steps, Crawford bent and picked up the leash and looped it over my arm. "If you decide to go," he said, "tie her up to something, maybe."

The dog tried to join them inside, but Brownie blocked her with his knee and closed the door behind him. Barkley and I stared at the quiet, nothing moving. I think we were watching for that big red door to fly open again, as if this were all some elaborate game.

But when nothing happened—and when nothing *kept* happening—I told the dog we'd be better without them. I clipped the leash to her collar and said I wasn't going to leave her. I led us out to the yard, saying for her to do her business, Barkley with her nose to the ground, lawn thick as suede, dog circling for some combination of feel and smell, the precise spot in the world to shit on.

It was a fine street with fine houses and fine young trees, a respite of yard, sun like a light bulb glowing behind the clouds. Even Lady B, Miss Barkingham, The Barkster, Barkalicious, she seemed content to take in the handsome stillness of the neighbors' lawns and driveways. She raised her nose to the air and turned back toward the house.

I realized I'd been holding my breath for the sound of the gun. Barkley and I could see into the living room through the picture window, the insides all dim and watery, ceiling made of cake frosting.

I said, "What do you think they're doing?"

I said, "Should we go in?"

She looked at me, and I asked if we should leave. We could walk to Michelle's house, I told her. No one would think of looking for us there. No one knew how I ran a mile and a half each way just to see the light in her window.

If we went to Michelle's, I said, we could be brave together and ring the doorbell. She might bring us inside, get us warm, give us something to eat. The dog knew what I was saying. Or at least she knew what my voice meant. We should have cut through the field, yet there we sat on the steps, Barkley slouching against me, her breath warm and swampy, the dog as heavy as a bag of sand against my leg. We watched the street, me asking if she could smell anyone on their way home.

She looked at me to say no.

She had slight shivers in her flanks, and I pulled her close to give her heat. I had the dog almost full on me now. She was short-haired and had zero reserves against the cool damp, her body with no stamina for this kind of waiting. I brushed the dog's ear against my face, chewed the felty tip lightly. I practiced like the dog was Michelle I was holding. I practiced talking quiet to her, saying it was nice to sit here together, saying she smelled good, saying it would be okay.

We had the street, the occasional bird coming and going, Barkley and I noticing nice things about the neighborhood to one another. The trees stood tidy and straight. If you closed your eyes and pictured a tree, these were the trees you'd see as sentinels in your mind. Nothing crisscrossed or carved for wires (like near my house), nothing spilling to the sidewalk all trashed and broken (like near Crawford's). Here things stood back austere and tended to, everything ordered, regimented, planned.

Such a good place for us to end up after school—food in fridge, sodas in basement, big flat yard. Even back then there had to be some bigger meaning to the lawns for me, that whole litany of good that seemed to fall so easily to streets like these, as if it was simply their due in life. The bounty never seemed to end.

No doubt it was more complicated, but how could I not have seen everything in terms of fathers? In my own little mousehood way, it was all about the presence (or the absence) of a father. This had to be the theme bubbling under the surface of everything for me. The finished basement, the woodstove, the Mustang half restored in the garage. Even the easy charm, the way Brownie could talk aloud without worry in class, the way he could take charge in a ballgame, it all had to come from somewhere.

Or, more to the point, it all had to come from someone.

Brownie's father stood as the most obvious difference between us that I could name. It was the only aspect I would have deliberately changed in my life if I could. Even if a father completely erased who I was at the time, and even if that man was no good to me at all, I'm positive I'd have traded everything for just the chance of a father. It wouldn't have even been a question.

The bristle of chin, the errands in town, that endless drudge of chores in the yard: how could I not feel that low-heat envy? How could everything not circle back again and again to that presence of a father (for someone like Brownie), or that absence of one (for kids like me and Crawford)?

One year I gave Brownie's father a Father's Day card. And how did that go over in their house, I wonder. Little Billy Buck, sweet and awkward, delivering this valentine to the man. What kind of lonely and misguided kid would think that was a good idea? Did they laugh after he was gone?

I might have been hungry or cold as I sat there with the dog. I might have been angry or hurt that Brownie left me out. I might have been worried about the gun. I might have moved through a hundred feelings, but one thing that was beyond any doubt was the yearning I felt for a father.

It came down to things as plain as the yard, or as ridiculous as ice skates, Brownie's father taking him every year to be fitted for a new pair. Langes, they were called—most killer skates ever—all molded and jet-fighter with ski-boot clasps. He'd have to keep rubber guards on the blades, Brownie and his father sharpening the metal edges on an electric grinder in the garage. His father told him the blades should be as sharp as barber's scissors.

My skates were these old leather and chrome monstrosities. Four sizes too big, they were steel-toed boots with long white laces that took years to tighten, especially if your ankles were bruised from the day before, and especially if you didn't quite know how to stop on ice. Any kid like me would have ceded all things hockey and baseball to Brownie, just as Brownie would donate earth sciences and American history to me. We'd divvy up the world, and I'd be the one who needed to do well in social studies and algebra. What else did I have? What else was an only child going to do when he got home but his homework?

It was just me and my mother and the television at night. In this way, people like Crawford and me would have been twins to each other. You could have gone through and circled every 'no' on a page—no father, no siblings, no garage, no go-carts, no trips to Florida—and you'd have thought all the negatives would add up to some extra bond for Crawford and me. You'd have thought we would be best friends, able to understand and appreciate each other, though maybe we matched up too perfectly. Maybe we cancelled each other out, Crawford and me having nowhere to go with one another, as if someone with the same story made your own less valuable, less your own.

• • •

Once, in Cub Scouts, our den mother gave us each a Pinewood Derby kit to take home. A blue box containing a block of wood, four wheels, four nails, my mother helping me to hammer it together on the kitchen table. We wrapped the car in tinfoil and painted lightning bolts on the side in red nail polish. It never entered our minds to round the edges or oil the wheels or glue pennies underneath for weight.

Downstairs in the church hall, that first glimpse of the other race cars, and it seemed a kind of beauty contest for fathers and sons. Brownie with that thin wedge of a car with retractable wings. My car on the table, and I heard someone ask whose dinner was defrosting. The hall went hot and crowded and airless, everyone talking at the same time.

Later, it would seem that everything a person would need to know about these boys could be found in that small tableau of pinewood cars. Nothing tragic, of course, but still, who'd expect little Billy Joe to keep coming back to the Cub Scouts after that?

There was the one time his mother arrived from work with a gift for him. Her kid should have something nice every now and then, she said—and she'd gone so far as to wrap the present, saying these had arrived in the store brand new that morning—and he opened and held the shirt up to his chest. It was bright orange, long-sleeved and silky, a kind of rayon with this motocross biker tearing life-sized across the front.

She asked if he liked it, and he told her no.

He said he didn't like the shirt at all.

He waited a moment.

And then he laughed and said he *loved* the shirt!

He danced around the kitchen table. He wore it to bed that night and wore it to school that next morning, tying his jacket around his waist so that everyone would know that orange sheen, the motocross guy ripping through mud.

He waltzed into homeroom only to find Crawford wearing the same exact shirt, same exact orange, same exact motocross guy. The two boys could have laughed or tried to joke it off. They could have paraded around as parallel universes to each other, soul mates coordinating their wardrobes the night before. But instead they stood stricken. They moved away from each other—diminished somehow—and neither of them ever wore the shirt to school again.

— 6 —

We sat on the steps, trying to be indifferent to the quiet and the cold, the dog and I just so beyond everything Brownie and Crawford might be doing inside. Let them have their secrets, we told each other. Let them have their warm house and food.

But then that click of door behind us, and we jumped back, dog starting to the door, Crawford stepping outside.

"Didn't mean to scare you," he said.

I pulled Barkley toward the yard, telling Crawford he didn't scare anyone. He closed the door and followed down the steps, me and Barkley on the grass watching for some hint of what had been going on inside, Crawford not quite looking at us, that lack of eyes meaning something.

I asked, "Did he show you the gun?"

"Is that what it is?" said Crawford.

I led the dog along the side of the house and said we'd found it on the way home after school. I told him we fired it down at the pond behind the cemetery.

"I thought something like that," said Crawford.

We stood on the front lawn, maybe an hour of afternoon left in the trees, and Crawford seemed to be doing the math in his head, saying, "That's what I'd have done."

There had to be more on his mind, but we were interrupted by a big blue Imperial coming over the crest of the street, the car turning into the Tanko driveway a half-dozen houses away. Barkley pulled toward the car. She pulled toward anything, but still no one noticed us down in the yard at the bottom of the street, like we were camouflaged with the shadows. Jenny and Adeana and their mother out of the car, voices chirpy and sparkling clear, girls home from swim or dance or whatever it was their parents provided.

Crawford and I stared as the lights went on in their house, room by room, the warmth of those clean big windows, the pastel walls inside. It left a kind of wistful longing, a pining for something we couldn't quite name. Such an assurance we felt that Jenny and Adeana would escape this town.

Cut to the dog pulling the other way against the leash. Cut to her trying to slip her collar, that big wolf whistle coming from the other side of the house, Brownie calling to us, and the dog leaning with all her weight against her neck. I wrapped the leather around my wrist, dog wheezing as she pulled, strangling herself to get to Brownie, Crawford giving me a look, like should we go?

Brownie must have come from the walk-out door of the basement, and Barkley cried each time she heard him, dog pulling around the side of the house, Brownie already to the back fence along the length of yard. He trusted we'd follow, didn't turn to look, that cool iron taste off the river, the dark glints of water through the trees, and Brownie sure of himself as he got toward the end of the fence.

The gate had a padlock, and we all knew the river was more than just verboten. It was one of the few completely off-limit things in our lives. It was nonnegotiable, yet there was Brownie with the key. He opened the lock and waited, Brownie picking at the green plastic on the fence. I wanted to see if there was a gun anymore. I wanted to see that weight inside his jacket. The dog tried ducking her head to get out of the collar, and I snapped down hard, telling her to stop already. Brownie turned to the sound and saw the dog curl small. He stood there and swung the gate open as we got to him.

"Shall we?"

What choice did we have? We bowed our heads and followed him single file through the gate. We went down the grassy path, down the stairs made of railroad ties, down to that wide spread of river. It was bright on the water, the current moving scary-fast, such raw power and force sweeping by. No wonder we weren't allowed anywhere near this place, the momentum almost pulling you in, almost urging you over the side, river sweeping behind Brownie, water the color of a magnet.

The dock—a kind of giant catapult of cables and planks and beams—jutted some twenty, twenty-five feet from the shore, phone poles driven perpendicular into the bank, river so close it seemed flush to the wood. His father must have built the dock some weekend with the help of buddies and equipment from work. How else to explain its existence?

The dog wanted no part of this. She had her instincts and moved as if afraid. Poor Barkley, needing to be with her boy out there, yet look how afraid she was to go anywhere near, bits of green and branches going left to right with the current, river so much faster than any of us could have run, Brownie already aboard the dock, those small tugs bouncing the wires, water catching the edge of the wood, whole rig trembling like a trap ready to spring. Brownie called for us to join him, called for the dog, me and Crawford trading looks again.

There was a hint of fresh-ploughed fields and manure in the water, and Brownie walked to the end of the dock and turned to us. Upriver there were trees cutting off the view, but downriver you could follow the long belly of cove and powdery light toward town. The water ran deep and flinty as it slowed and deepened toward the dam at Belding's. It would flow over the dam and continue past the shopping center, flowing under one, two, three bridges, carp and weeds above the falls, the river sliding past the smell of paint, past that growing taste of potato chips toward the next town south.

Crawford followed Brownie onto the dock. He turned midway on the planks over the water to check on me and Barkley, to see if we were coming, that tepid half smile of his. At first the dog and I didn't move from the ledge of shore, but then Brownie called again, and she stepped onto the wood, Brownie standing behind Crawford at the far end, the two of them over the river, me and Barkley coming to join them. We were all aboard this little ship now, Brownie bouncing the dock, the dog crouching, her nails trying to grab at the planks.

I always thought it would be more of a moment.

I always pictured everything bigger and better than it was.

It was crude and abrupt, the way Brownie lifted his jacket to show the pistol. The gun black against the soft pale of his stomach. The pistol tucked into the belt of his pants. It was the head of a snake poking out. It was the beak of a bird. Even if you expected to see all along the exact thing he had in his hand right now, even if you could still feel that gyroscopic cling of this object from earlier, it would take a moment to recognize, Brownie taking the gun from his waist and holding it out to us. He pulled back on the slide, that visceral lock step of machinery as he eased the magazine out from the bottom of the grip.

He was showing off, flashing the bullets, closing the clip back into the handle with the heel of his hand. He moved toward Crawford and offered the gun like a dare, saying, "Here you go, Breeze."

Crawford turned, his eyes asking me what to do, and I said, "Don't look at me, I'm not the one with the gun."

Brownie pushed the gun onto him.

Crawford turned to Brownie, and I couldn't see their faces anymore. That whorl of hair on the back of Crawford's head like a hurricane spinning. Brownie clicked the safety and started to count down from ten, nine—a long time passed—and I tried to say something, tried to say stop, but nobody seemed to hear me. Perhaps I wasn't really speaking, Crawford putting out his hand for the gun.

— 7 —

In my fantasy version of us, we would forever come back to the river. It would be after college, after wives and kids, after regular jobs and lives, after we'd become the people we needed to be. I always pictured us meeting up from time to time out on the dock with a few beers. Our victory lap, that huge mass of water passing between the banks, that soothing view of river and cove, our little hometown glowing and tame in the distance. And somewhere in the vicinity of this dream, lying dormant in the mud at the bottom of the river, would be the gun we threw away. You could almost see it there. It would sink into the layers of sediment. It would become a fossil hidden in rock. And the river would become this charmed thing for us. Its waters would hold our secret. We would have survived. A certain serenity would be ours. We would have been able to rest.

You might think a person could tell anything he wanted—lie to his heart's content, make it all up—as if anyone would know the difference, as if anyone would truly care. Honestly, couldn't someone take the raw material of their lives and just alter it slightly, just enough to make things turn out better for them? Who'd begrudge these kids coming out on the other side of this day strong and self-assured?

Such small adjustments it would have taken. So minor the changes to make things good for them. Yet the truth seemed to have its own requirements, didn't it? We were small fish in a small pond, and every time we tried to pretend otherwise we went flat and lifeless. The things that happened had a kind of specific gravity. Events had a kind of substance, a kind of stubbornness that resisted you, reality having a will all its own

I'd try as hard as I could, but I'd not be able to change a single thing about what happened. I couldn't so much as change our names. Sorry, Crawford. Sorry, Mr. and Mrs. Brownell. Sorry, Tom and Michelle and Dave and Chubs. Sorry, Rodney Sellers. Sorry, Ginny Markowitz, wherever you are. We really did play this dopey game of How Many Babies with you. Just as Brownie and I really did make a second science project—*ALL THINGS RIVER*—a sequel to our pond, the two of us naming everything found in a river.

We memorialized our river, from the wastewater treatment plant to the hydro-electric dam. We included the flood of our town in 1955: Hurricane Connie, Hurricane Diane, the magnesium plant fire, half the houses washed away. We pasted in pictures. We included postcards of the falls and mills. We embellished our margins with Mark Twain—thank you, Crawford—and I borrowed a fancy calligraphy pen from my mother for the quotes we used:

We had mighty good weather, as a general thing, and nothing ever happened to us at all—that night, nor the next, nor the next.

And:

If you tell the truth, you don't have to remember anything.

And there it was in writing—a path forward in the story—no need to remember anything, if you only trusted yourself to what really happened. And since you could not lift one solitary thing away from these kids, since you could not seem to improve or rearrange or edit any of what took place, the only way to understand an afternoon like this was to let the facts speak for themselves, allow them to say what they needed to say.

Instead of reaching back to save these boys, perhaps it's these doomed boys reaching forward to save you. Maybe that's why you can't seem to change anything, because they're not allowed to change anymore. They're not the ones at stake in this. It's no longer possible for them to be different. If anything, they're the ones whispering forward to you. They're the ones trying to help you feel your way through.

Despite every wish, Brownie never threw the gun. He never did anything even close to that. All of us stuck to the script, Crawford's long and slender fingers wrapped around the barrel. He admired the pistol in his hand. He said it'd be a good color for a bike. He touched the sharp cuts in the metal.

I had a twinge of jealousy.

More than a twinge, I yearned to be Crawford, to be as normal and easy, to be him turning the pistol in his hands without any hesitations or qualms, like it was no big deal, Brownie saying the gun wasn't locked. Crawford pointed away and down from us, away from me and Brownie, away from the dog.

Brownie told Crawford to shoot the gun if he wanted.

"Okay," said Crawford—and he looked upstream, the gun following the direction of his eyes. He didn't belabor any of this, Crawford aiming off toward that hazy curtain of trees upstream, his feet set strong and solid.

The shot went off—some kid with a firecracker—big bang that was gone almost instantly, absorbed into the wideness of river and sky, a cottony quiet, the dog pulling back with fear, Brownie with a smile suspended as if in awe. Crawford examined the gun in his hand, weighing it, not looking to either me or Brownie. Instead he tracked a clot of leaves floating past and pulled the trigger again—loud and close, a small rip of splash, and the case plinking to the dock and into the water—and the dog kept trying to slip her collar to get away from the gun.

Crawford was on a roll, pointing at the river, pressing the trigger, the sound smaller and more compact, Brownie moving forward, motioning for him to stop. I thought he was protecting the dog from the noise, Barkley desperate to get away, her nails scrabbling on the wood, and me almost falling into the water. I pulled on her angrily, wanting her to stop, wanting Crawford to stop, wanting everyone to stop, Brownie yelling something to Crawford.

When Crawford didn't seem to hear, Brownie grabbed at his arm and another shot went off.

The bullet panged straight down.

It went straight into the wood of the dock.

The plank was splintered, like it had exploded.

We checked ourselves.

We checked each other.

We patted our chests and arms.

We were safe and alive and had those holy-shit grins on our faces to one another. Crawford handed the gun back to Brownie slow and formal, like it was some dramatic moment, the transfer of this sacred object.

Brownie stood against the waning light with the gun. He gave that one furtive glimpse back, that sly grin, and then he turned and aimed at the river, the three of us waiting—Crawford, Barkley, me—and still he was not able to pull the trigger. It was awful, and I felt sorry for him. I felt sorry for all of us, the gun hanging at Brownie's side, me and Crawford exchanging looks.

It was here that Crawford lifted his face to the air upstream, him putting out his hand and saying to listen. Hard to hear anything, those after-hum pistol shots in our ears like cicadas. The dog cocked her head toward the sound, a kind of unquiet coming to us. It might have been a trick of the wind, like sleigh bells at first, like accordion music in the distance.

It was a pair of ducks, two of them flying low along the dark of the shoreline toward us. Their wings tipped into the water as they flew, leaving small brief circles on the surface, and we could hear the effort, that hiss of feathers as they got closer, one bird following a few feet behind the other, each passing no more than a dozen yards from the end of the dock, green iridescent head of the male, soft brown belly of the female.

Without thinking, I said, "Steven!"

I said, "The birds!"

As if he didn't know.

As if he wouldn't have raised the pistol without me.

As if they weren't slightly past the dock by now, but still near enough for him to shoot, the ducks fading down the river. Another moment and they would be too far.

Brownie would be the last to look away, gun pointing down, birds vanishing in the gray green of the cove. He'd be watching when nothing was there anymore. The dog would shake her collar, and Brownie would turn to us, and then what would happen? Would we come forward to help? Would we try to do anything good for him?

No, our first reaction—or *my* first reaction, at least—was to laugh in his face.

I said to Crawford, "Look at him!"

In all the years I knew Brownie—in all the ways I would remember him— I cannot recall ever once seeing him cry. I knew him angry and exhausted and hungover, knew him funny and loyal and hurt and helpful and generous to a fault. Brownie high-as-a-kite, Brownie in all of his glory, as well as all of his blowhard failure. But I never knew him in tears. This moment was the closest. Gun in his hand, face slack, he seemed lost out there on the dock. I wanted to taunt him for this. I wanted to say how bored I was by him. I wanted to loom over my friend here, tease Brownie back to himself.

I called him a loser.

He nodded and said he agreed.

The dog must have heard the strain in his voice, the way she pulled to him again.

And even as I was doing it I was wondering what took me so long to let go of the leash. I dropped that soft loop of leather. I let her go where she wanted, Barkley starting over the wooden planks to him, the water sweeping under, leash slithering across the dock.

She passed Crawford, and Brownie talked to her, his voice soft. She fought to keep herself moving, dog crouching as she stepped over the gaps in the planks, Brownie reaching for her as she got close. He leaned down to scratch her ear, her neck.

Crawford dug for the watch under the cuff of his jacket, and Brownie looked up and asked what time was it?

It was just after five, said Crawford—and he looked upriver—and Brownie suggested there could be more birds.

Crawford said no.

We stared at him.

Crawford said that birds flying low meant rain.

We asked how he knew such a thing.

Crawford said, "Jim says it to Huck on the river."

"And you remember?" asked Brownie.

"I do," said Crawford.

And Crawford was so sincere that we smiled. We took a moment to appreciate him. We let there be time for the river to swirl past, time for us to feel what it was to be safe and healthy, time for a deep breath before Brownie turned and fired the gun.

—8—

The pistol went off in his hand—loud and final—and when we saw one another still here, a kind of nervous relief started giggling up out of us, Crawford breaking into a jitterbug dance, the dock bounding, me with my arms up for Brownie! Hurrah! Victory!

The dock could have sailed away, we were so happy. Instead of all the things we did wrong, we could set about naming the many things we did right: we'd shot the gun, we'd carried it through town, we'd not killed one another. We could henceforth assume the best in ourselves. Even the sun seemed to come out. One last salute, the undersides of the clouds tinged with pink, a church ceiling.

I said, "And what was so hard about that?"

I don't think any of us noticed the dog.

The next thing we knew was the slump of her body.

There was a quiet leaning, and then she just slipped into the river, her body pressing tight to the upside edge of the dock.

Brownie had the leash, but she was being pulled under by the current, the river tugging her down, her body curling, mouth stretched, eyes wide, gun in Brownie's hand. He was hanging her, the dog unable to breathe.

Crawford joined at side of the dock and grabbed the scruff of the dog's neck.

I was watching, Crawford on his knees, his sleeves wet to the elbows, Brownie pulling hard on the leash, the two of them trying to keep her above the surface, but then the line went empty and loose, and she slipped Crawford's hand, Brownie holding that hollow loop of collar, the dog not anywhere. She was gone. Nothing but river swirling, the water like cellophane in the light.

We didn't have time to panic, the dog appearing twenty or thirty yards downstream, forelegs splashing, river carrying her away faster than seemed possible. I think we thought any moment she'd start swimming to shore. I think we were expecting her to right herself, the dog sweeping out toward the middle of the river, her head a dot on the cove some fifty, seventy, a hundred yards away. We glanced at each other. We thought maybe she'd make it to the other side. I looked for blood on the wood of the dock.

"She'll catch on the dam," said Crawford.

"We can cut through the field," said Brownie, already moving.

He was midway on the dock, gun in one hand, leash in the other, and Crawford brushed past me, Brownie coming up behind him, me stepping in front of him, me stopping Brownie before he could get by.

"What are you doing?" he asked.

"Your hand," I told him.

I had to point it out for him to see—gun in one hand, leash in the other—and he gave me the collar, the leather cold and solid as a snake. Brownie lifted his shirt and tucked the gun in his belt, pushing the barrel into his pants. He pulled his coat flat, like he was good at this now. He patted his belly and started toward the steps.

I followed up to the yard, Crawford waiting at the gate for us, everything darker away from the river, the three of us crossing the lawn in the shadow of the house, and this small squeak of a voice freezing us in an instant.

We stopped right there.

It was sharp and sweet and unmistakable, Brownie's brother rambling on and on to their mother, the kitchen door standing open at the back deck. The lights went on in the dining room windows. Brownie's mother passed into the house carrying grocery bags, little Tommy coming out onto the back deck, that trill of boy jabbering away to his mother, Mrs. Brownell appearing in the doorway, her heels hollow on the wood as she crossed to the edge of the deck.

She was slim and young in slacks, short dark hair, and she knocked the crusts and crumbs from the boy's lunchbox at the railing. We hadn't moved. We might have blended into the yard. Our most desperate hope: that she might not even notice, Tommy distracting her from the doorway, Brownie standing perfectly still, no one here to see, nobody on the lawn.

"Hello, boys," she said, her voice tipping up as if amused, as if curious what we were up to this time.

Such a different world she was in, his mother standing on the deck over us. We must have struck her as funny, the three of us frozen, that smile of hers not expecting anything bad. To her we were still good kids in the midst of some kind of mischief.

"What are you up to?" she asked.

"Five more minutes," said Brownie.

She closed the lunchbox and told him no.

"Please, Mom," he said.

And she must have heard something she didn't like in his voice, because her face seemed to tighten. She stopped and studied him more closely. She studied all of us. She said, "It's time, Steven."

She said, "It's time, all of you."

She had dinner on the table, she said, and still Brownie begged to let us go for just a minute.

We looked to each other. We could have run straight to the mill and the dam. No one could stop us. We had that urge in our legs. We could have gone to the dog. We could hear Tommy's voice calling from inside the house. Mrs. Brownell must have seen the hesitation between us, and she worried the metal latch on the lunchbox, as if to say it was not an option, whatever we were up to.

"Steven Mark," she said, "up here now."

She wasn't talking to me or Crawford, but all we could do was obey and start toward the house. It was like we were chained together. All I could manage was to walk in the footsteps of Crawford. And how quick we were to abandon the dog. All it took was a step toward the house for us to become two-faced and self-dealing, like we'd been faking our care and loyalty all along. I wanted to change that fact. I wanted to go after her myself. Why should something as slight as dinner on the table matter? How could that ever stop us?

Our mascot, our good-luck charm, our brindle-ginger girl: we'd sell her out in a minute, like whatever we said or felt added up to nothing at all, like there was no higher calling to anything.

You could feel Brownie sag, him and Crawford and me in a line walking up toward the deck, Tommy there with his mother as we arrived. He was her favorite by far, Tommy a thick-set, blonde-haired version of his brother, smaller and softer, sweeter and less tough, yet those same straight-across bangs, same hatchet chin, freckles, dimples.

At seven years old Tommy pressed himself shy against her, half behind, half into Mrs. Brownell's legs, thumb in his mouth.

Right away on the deck she saw the empty leash in my hand. The length of dark leather, that tink of tags at the collar: how could she miss any of it? We were in front of her, as if standing for inspection, my chin starting to go all quicksand. I hated the way my face always had to get away from me. I looked down at her shoes. Tan, practical, with heels, the toes turning on the deck toward Brownie, Tommy's sneakers following, his mother's voice asking where was the dog?

"We were down at the dock," he told her.

"And what happened, Steven?"

"She got loose," he said.

"What's that mean?"

"I don't know, Mom."

"She'll be at the dam," I said.

"No one goes near that river," said his mother. "Do you hear me?"

She looked each of us in the eye.

She said, "Say it back to me."

We told her that no one goes near the river, our voices almost nonexistent, Mrs. Brownell asking again what happened, each of us saying we weren't sure what happened.

"She just fell into the water," said Brownie.

There was that break in his voice again, and you could see he wasn't lying.

"It's true," I said.

And she shushed me.

She shushed all of us. She had no tolerance for anything like this, and I saw Brownie adjust the gun under his coat. He still had the pistol. He still had that to carry. He seemed to wither under the weight, his mother in front of him, that stare of hers.

I could feel it.

I had the leash in my hands.

I was wringing it, saying all of a sudden, "It was me, Mrs. Brownell.

Saying, "I did it."

I looked her straight and unwavering and said, "I was the one who lost the dog."

She seemed to consider this for a moment, which seemed an opening for me, my cue, my place to step in and start crying.

Or to start *not* crying, more like it.

That'd be my one stroke of brilliance for the day: I'd have Mouse holding back that deluge of tears, mouth like a sock puppet of emotions folding toothless on itself, poor kid playing the sad little fatherless card yet again. We'd be golden here. We'd be hitting all the friendship and sympathy buttons.

I must have realized his mother could forgive or blame me in ways that she'd never be able to forgive or blame her own son. I alone could do this for him: my gift to Steven. Mouse could be the bad one here. I could be the reason for everything, the one who made this terrible thing happen.

She'd want to protect Tommy from this.

It'd be too embarrassing, too painful to watch.

She'd clap her hands to scatter the moment, Mrs. Brownell turning to Crawford, saying, "You're being awfully quiet over there, Crawford—everything okay?"

He'd say, "I just feel bad."

"It's probably fine," she'd tell him, saying the dog went on these little adventures all the time.

He'd say, "Yes, Ma'am."

She'd say, "I'll bet she's home before you even get to your houses."

We'd all feel the lie of this, just as we'd all know that the less we talked the better. We'd stand on the deck until the woman dismissed us, Mrs. Brownell saying we should be getting home.

"I'll have Steven call you tonight," she'd tell us. "After dinner, after we find her."

She'd clap again to get us to move. It'd be getting dark, sun down, clouds close and low again, and Brownie lifting the leash from me. We'd start around to the front yard, Tommy tagging along with us, and Mrs. Brownell going into the warm of the house.

It'd be Tommy who asked if the dog was okay. It'd be his little voice that asked if she was hurt, or if she was killed, or if she was coming back.

No one said goodbye so much as just slowly drifted apart. Crawford and I started up the hill, Brownie and Tommy staying back in the turnaround. The lawn looked silver behind us, our footprints a swath of dark. Brownie went with his brother toward the side of the house, the young boy calling into the dusk for the dog. We could hear that voice of his. We could see the two of them submerged down there, the little boy singing for Barkley, Mrs. Brownell on the front steps, her arms folded, and the fire station horn going off—three long tones echoing high then low—the town calling its young ones home, finally, saying, *"Come home...*

"Come home...

"Come home...."

Just enough daylight for us to get back to where we belonged, the driveways and trees collecting the dark now, clots of night in the branches, Crawford and I passing the bright warm windows of the Tanko house up the street. We took one last look down to Brownie, but he and his brother were gone, the front steps empty, the house sitting as if at the bottom of a lake.

He would still have to manage the gun. He would need to keep his brother safe. The drop ceiling in the basement, the crawlspace behind the bathtub: only so many places you could hide a thing like this. His whole life it would sit there and weigh on him, just like his mother's silence would weigh on him, just like his father's arriving home any minute would weigh on him.

But that would be later. At the moment though, the house would be so quiet and barren without the dog, his brother crying, his mother simmering at the window, Crawford and I simply walking away.

At the turn to Church Street, we caught that first rattle of diesel, Brownie's father coming around the corner. We could have crouched behind some parked car, but then it was too late, me and Crawford caught in the headlights, the man slowing as he pulled up to us.

"Billy Buck!" he said.

"Crawfman!" he said.

"What's the word, guys?"

There was no word—and we stared at him without saying anything—and he gave us that uneasy grin, like he was concerned about us, we were so out of the running in life, like we were so completely over our heads. Couldn't even say hello normal, Brownie's father waving us along, saying get home safe.

We could have done the rest of the walk in our sleep—past St. Mary's, past the barbershop. We had mothers waiting for us. We knew their fear would soon turn to anger, their anger melting down to a sort of overkindness, a sort of neediness that made them pry about our friends, about our days at school, about our feelings.

We got to the row houses where Crawford lived, and he slowed and said he could walk me only as far as here.

"That's fine," I said.

"You okay?" he asked.

"I am," I said.

But then how bad must I have been? How much of a mess must this have been, if someone like Crawford felt the need to take care of me? We arrived at his front steps, the windows upstairs with those pale yellowed curtains, lights on in the rooms.

He should go up, he told me.

Even his voice was deeper. Still those strong white teeth, him smiling weakly, Crawford like a version of the man he'd become: skin darker, hair tighter and shinier, face lined and taut. I put out my hand to shake with him. It was awkward, the gesture, as if the two of us were agreeing on something.

I held the rail and watched him go.

"See you tomorrow," I called.

He waved and went on. Tomorrow he'd be that much bigger, almost unrecognizable from the boy we first lured from the steps. Soon he'd start wearing pomade in his hair. He'd tell us not to call him Breeze anymore. He'd stand there to make sure we heard him, his voice deep and serious. Behind his back he was still Breeze, still Bimini, but no one called him anything but Crawford to his face. He'd be stronger and faster and angrier. He'd become all muscle and athlete, playing basketball, running track.

Not long from these steps, he'd have girlfriends and part-time jobs and plans for the Service. But for now I watched him open the door to the downstairs lobby, saw him pass the mailboxes and climb the stairs. It seemed he was being lifted away.

A mist was falling through the lights—the rain coming—and I stood in the street and stared up at the windows. The drizzle fell heavier. I stayed where I was and let the cold and dark creep slowly into me. I put my mittens on. I wanted Crawford to remember the way he shot the gun. I wanted him confident and defiant, him showing us how to be good and smart in the world. I wanted him sitting down to a warm meal with his mother. I wanted Crawford untroubled, untouched by anything from this day, him reading his books, his mother singing along with her records long into the night.

She had a deep, lovely voice. She'd wanted to be a professional singer. Crawford had told me this once. She met his father and things turned out different than she planned. Now she had swing shifts at American Optical, which meant every three weeks Crawford and his mother would be on the same timetable. That must have been a nice stretch in the schedule for them, something they looked forward to (first shift). Other weeks he'd be alone for dinner and bedtime (second shift). And other weeks he'd have to sleep in an empty apartment (third shift). Every creak and noise must have woken him during those times, Crawford alone, the night dark and quiet. If he was lucky, his mother would arrive in time to see him off for school.

    I'd forget that I was standing in the rain, but then I'd become aware of Crawford in a movement of curtains upstairs, his shape dark behind the glass. My friend looked down, the rain coming steady now, and this little kid on the street staring up at the window as if lovesick.

— 9 —

Once upon a time there was a boy heading home in the rain. It was late for him, almost dark, cars passing on the street with their headlights, the cemetery with its sea bottom of stones, and those big hunchback willows. The Chevelle in the driveway, the pale light over the patio, meaning his mother would be pacing the kitchen.

She'd always expect the worst. Her father died when she was five years old, and her whole life would have to rhyme with this fact: his mother as a girl coloring in the living room in Bayside with her sister, the front door banging open, winter air gushing, snow tracked down the hall to the bedroom, her father on the floor.

Staring at his own house in the darkness, the boy knew what awaited him there. She'd be angry if he was late, though she could never be angry for long. It wasn't in the budget. He was all that she had in the world. He knew and used this as a tool. It made him less nice, less the good son, and more and more like the person he thought he would have to be in order to survive.

He could put off going home. He could press against the granite stones of the wall to lessen the rain, that lonely cold crawling into him. No one would see him here, the boy full of dread, afraid to go home, afraid to stay out.

And what, exactly, would dread feel like again?

Dread, it seemed, would be cold and wet and tired behind the eyes, skin sensitive to the touch. It would leave this scoured feel inside his stomach like a fist clenching. Dread would procrastinate him toward the lights of Cumberland Farms. It would wander him through the sliding doors, the girl behind the counter barely lifting her eyes from her magazine as he passed into the warmth. The racks of cigarettes, the spools of lottery tickets, the hum of fluorescent lights. Dread being that wet-cardboard smell of burned coffee. Dread being the bullet in his pocket. One could almost forget it was there. One could almost forget the entire day after school, dread becoming the hot dogs rolling under heat lamps, the eyes of the girl at the register, like what was he doing here? Why was he bothering her? Dread was him drifting along the glass of the dairy freezer, along the shelves of snack cakes, this kid with a Slim Jim in his hand, the boy snaking it up the sleeve of his jacket, and then floating back out into the rain, in no hurry as he walked home.

199 WOODSTOCK AVENUE, and the house was unbreathably warm for a boy coming home, sautéed onions in a pan on the stove, his mother taking one look and telling him to get out of those wet clothes. She'd have dinner ready as soon as he was in his pajamas. A good son could have told her why he was late. A good mother could have known and asked the right question. Even if it was a complete lie, the two of them could have found ways to make each other's lives easier. He could have washed the dishes after supper. He could have stayed in the kitchen with her to talk. He could have offered to help soak her feet, pouring fresh warm water in the basin, sprinkling Epsom salt.

A bad son would eat in front of the television. He would pretend not to wait for the phone to ring, not to think of them, Brownie and his father riding in the truck, the two of them looking through town for the dog. They'd see every shadow as her.

And when the phone rang that night, he jumped to answer. Only it was his aunt from Staten Island. He barely said hello, bringing the receiver to the kitchen to his mother. She cupped the mouthpiece and whispered for him to get her a towel. He got down on his knees and tamped her ankles dry with a dishcloth. The pain in those feet pulled some rope in his stomach, those deep-cut marks from her shoes, her bunions glowing red from standing all day.

As she talked to her sister, he tried to will her off the phone—think how expensive the long distance was, feel how tired she had to be after work. Even with him hovering near her, even with her shooing him away, she and her sister could talk for hours, entire paychecks going to the phone company, his mother and her sister laughing and chatting about nothing.

Throat sore, face warm, the boy would drift away to his room and listen from down the hall, her voice murmuring along with the television. Hard to follow what she was saying, yet in that hush he knew they were talking about the palm reader again.

They had gone together last Christmas. The boy had heard the story a hundred times. An old man at a table held them gently by the fingers and told the sisters how their father died when they were young, one of the girls with a scar on her thigh from a glass box of crayons that broke in the commotion of doctors and neighbors that day. The man told how each of their marriages had ended (or was ending).

And enough of what he said had come true to scare them. They had the cassette as proof—and the palm reader explained how unlucky they were going to be with love and money, and how each had a major misfortune coming: one of them dying from some variety of hemorrhage very soon, and the other having all her teeth extracted before her next birthday. Not a nice fortune to look forward to, nothing hopeful, which only made them believe and fear and remember what he said all the more.

It was too late to call Brownie by the time she got off the phone and came down the hall to find him in his room, the boy sitting at his desk as if practicing being at school. He pretended to be busy over some kind of school project. She told him it was time for bed and continued down the hall to the bathroom. He could follow her by the sounds alone, her weight over that crackle of linoleum, his mother rooting through the drawers at the vanity. Was she looking into the mirror? Was she sitting on the toilet?

He pretended to be working as she made her way back toward his room. He pretended to be busy with papers, as if he hadn't noticed she was there in his doorway.

"Everything okay?" she asked.

He said he was fine.

"Anything you want to tell me?"

He shook his head no.

She stood framed in the light, and he felt her eyes press on him as she leaned against the door, his mother waiting for him to turn. She moved closer to him and opened her hand and asked what was this?

Took him a moment—small brass gleam in her palm—so interesting to see this bullet cupped in her hand. Could have been a coin or pebble, some leftover remnant of a dream, this little nugget arriving.

"It was in your pocket," she said.

"I know," he told her.

"Where'd you get it?"

"We found it."

"You and Steven?"

"Yes," he said.

"On the way home from school?"

"Yes," he said.

She closed her hand into a fist.

"What were you going to do with it?" she asked.

"I don't know," he said. "Nothing."

She stared at him, as if to ask where he'd learned to lie like this.

"Mind if I keep it?" she asked.

"I don't care," he told her.

He had memorized that saving power of quiet, and the boy stared as she handed him a folded square, tiny packet sealed neatly on itself, saying she found this in his pants, too. He didn't have to look. It'd be from Michelle, paper lavender in color, slightly damp, note folded in the elaborate way that girls sent letters in school.

His mother handed this to him along with a Slim Jim, which she said she found on the floor, his mother watching as he tossed both of these things to the desk, like he couldn't be bothered, like it couldn't be less important to him. She tried to talk to him, tried to open him up, but he wouldn't let this happen, boy moving away, his mother saying lights off in five minutes as she went back down the hall.

He followed with his ears as she went to her room. He listened as she opened the jewelry box on her dresser, where she kept her rings and bracelets, necklaces, newspaper clippings, report cards from school, and now a bullet. She'd go to the living room from there. The rain would tap on the window. He would stare and hear her in the kitchen. Phone on the wall, dial tone there if someone lifted the receiver, but there'd be no call from Brownie, no telephone ringing.

When he knew his mother was settled in the kitchen at the table, when he knew she had safely started her coffee mug full of wine, he reached for the note on his desk. The lettering had bled from the rain or the woods—*FOR BILL ONLY*, with a heart around it—and he carefully unfolded the paper, that slight smell of bubble gum (real or imagined), Michelle's handwriting soft and bubbly with loops and circles. The note arrived to him here like a message from another life:

> *Hi Billy Joe!*
>
> *What's up? Nothing much here! So, which side of the coin did it turn out? To be a sweetheart or not to be a sweetheart? (I hope it was sweetheart!) After fourth period when we go to homeroom are you going to wait to see me? Why were you trying to hide in study hall? You don't like me staring at you? My father and mother might take me out to dinner tonight, but I'm not*

sure. Are you and your mother getting along better? I hope so, because she might ground you and then I will never see you again. I can't see the clock, but I think it's almost time for the bell to ring. Catch ya later! Write back soon!
        XOXO, Mich Marie

  The rain would continue, the boy in bed. He could feel the house tremble, threads connecting to wherever his mother moved, the television under everything.

  He would not be a good sleeper this night. Lying in the dark, half of him would want nothing to happen. Let the moment pass. Just fall asleep. But then the other half would want some kind of visitation. He would want someone tapping at the glass, scratching at the screen for him to open the window. He would let the quiet linger heavy until some presence arrived in a gust of rain.

  He'd switch on the light and enact his little Mouse ways. Nearly all his life he'd do this, scuttle around the room all hours, his collections to rearrange and touch into order. What a kid, perfectly self-contained, taking care of these things—the bottle caps, the loose nails, pull tabs, books on the shelves, boxes under the bed—his primary job in the world to keep all these misfit objects and make them feel safe and useful.

  At some point in the night he must have gone to sleep, because he would wake again to darkness, the static of rain, the acid burn of guilt for that day, him and Brownie, and then Crawford, and then Barkley somewhere out in the night. The dog would come back in dreams, but they would never find her.

He'd have to know this, eventually. He'd have to admit as much to himself. He'd lie there, straining to hear his mother. She'd be in her bedroom (her breaths like those waves rolling into shore), or she'd be in her chair in the living room (where she often fell asleep on her way to bed), or she'd be in the kitchen (where she sat as a night owl at the table). The fear underneath everything was that she wouldn't be there anymore.

He'd live in fear that he'd be alone.

He'd get up to go find her.

The television would be on, volume low, and she'd be in the living room, sleeping in her chair. He'd have to lean close to make sure she was breathing. Always a relief, her chest moving, her breaths shallow and quiet. He'd lay an afghan over her.

Then he'd go into the bathroom. He'd stand at the toilet and pee. He'd take the aftershave from the shelf. It had been his father's—bright blue liquid—and the boy would unscrew the cap to get that sharp medicine smell. He'd put the cap back on and angle the aftershave where he knew his mother would see it there, where she'd think it odd, the way this thing had arrived to this place, as if the object had stepped off that footprint of dust for some reason.

The hand that did this sort of thing would not be his. The entity that moved the bottle would not be him. He'd swear on his life that he was nowhere near this place. He'd promise on his father's grave that it was not him gliding past her in the living room. No way would it be him edging into the kitchen to unbury an old bottle of whiskey from under the sink. How would a bottle find its way out from among those cleaners and chemicals? It'd be half full of rusty liquid—that yellow Fleischmann's label positioned for anyone to see—his father's bottle at the front of the cabinet.

The clock, the stove, the table and chairs, they would witness what kind of apparition had been here. They would be able to tell her what kind of force had been at work in this place. Later, when she was alone in the stillness, he imagined the faucet would be there to drip, drip, drip at her. That pecking of the water, slow and steady, would try to get through, try to tell her how something had visited in the night.

A kind of demon had been at work in this house, some sort of energy drifting past as she slept, and she'd seem to remember a chill in the night, the way she found the afghan up to her chin, and this vague movement of shadow down the hall as she half woke, half dreamed. A phantom would slip into her bedroom, that slow click of the bedside light going on, and this quiet opening of the jewelry box on the dresser. Two skinny fingers would stir the bullet in among the silver coins.

There'd be an old newspaper clipping—an advertisement for two-trouser suits on one side, an obituary on the other. Something to hold for a moment, if only to make the record complete, if only to document the things that disappear, something to stare at and hold more than read:

> WILLIAM STEVEN LYCHECK [sic]—*of Holton Road, North Franklin, died Sunday evening unexpectedly. He was born in North Franklin, July 1, 1925, son of the late William and Rosie (Palomar) Lycheck. He had been a resident of Cargill Falls and made his home in North Franklin for the past six years. He*

operated a window cleaning service in Cargill Falls. He was a veteran of World War Two, served in the Pacific in the Marine Corps 1943-46. Surviving are one son, William J. of Cargill Falls; one brother, Daniel J. of North Franklin; two sisters, several nieces and nephews. Visitation hours from 6 to 9 p.m., July 29, Leffler Funeral Home. (Reception at the Ukrainian National Home, located by the Little League fields).

And these tiny claws would gently drape this yellowed slip of paper atop the pile. The lid of the box about to be carefully closed. And from out of nowhere some new photo, an old black-and-white snapshot, a man half naked in a kitchen.

It would arrive like a splash of water, and the boy would be abruptly awake. The claws would be gone. The energy would have flown away.

Not once had he ever imagined his father being silly and fun. Not once did he brush up against the man laughing.

Never once did he think of his father as drunk or funny or playful.

It'd be a loud picture, the man roaring up like a walrus. Imperfect but happy. His father with those old gone cabinets, the countertops, the bottle, electric cord, socks, calendar. This poor excuse of a father finding his way to her jewelry box, the bastard (my mother's word), this glorious jerk standing so triumphant atop it all. Surprise! Hurrah! There he'd be for her, the very first thing she'd find when she opened that wooden chest of hers.

―PART THREE―

— I —

They found him in a motel room out by Alexander's Lake. Someone had seen his pickup truck in the parking lot and called his wife, Brenda. She said she knew right away, right when the phone rang, and she had them break the door down to get to him. He'd propped a desk chair under the handle. His body was in the bathroom—light on, fan humming—and back in the room by the bed he'd left a note.

She didn't keep what he wrote, she said. She didn't want to have him in her mind that way. It wasn't him talking anymore. He must have started in with everything, words slurring off the page by the end, this hurt and meanness coming out of him. He had that side, no need to deny it, but she told me that was between him and her now, which meant it was as good as gone from the world.

There were things no one else would ever know, she said. Not even his mother or father would need the details. None of it would help anyone feel better about anything.

The Comfort Inn and Suites at Killingly, off Attawaugan Crossing. It could have been anywhere, just one of those anonymous hotel rooms, except for that constant smell of potato chips, and except for the fact that he was close enough to walk home to his wife and daughter in one direction, and close enough to walk to his mother and father in the other. He had his pill crusher with him. He had vodka, limes, Chinese take-out, beer, candy bars, bananas: his whole package in a grocery box. No gun involved, no blood, no violence, just Brownie half naked on a bathroom floor. They found him curled around the toilet, his body all bloated and pale, his face like bread in water.

He was supposed to be on a business trip. Brownie ran his own logistics company, though the details always seemed sketchy. Even the two box trucks he leased, the small warehouse, the fat clip of cash he carried in his pocket at all times. They'd find that he'd incinerated all his papers. They'd say that he must have had tax problems, or drug problems, or health issues, as though there were one string to connect all the streaming shadows. They'd say he always had some scheme going: a rental property with his father, an offer to take over some auto parts franchise, some linen service. Brownie always one opportunity away, one yes from being set for good.

He called his parents that afternoon. He left a message at a time he knew they'd not be home. Nothing unusual about him saying hello. He'd sound normal enough, unless you went endlessly listening for signs of what lay a few hours ahead, Brownie saying it was only him checking in. He said to take care of each other.

He called Brenda that night, asking if everything was all right, if she was hanging in there at home. He said he was somewhere outside Philadelphia, some random motel. Such a good liar he was, right down to all the construction, the traffic outrageous on 95, Brownie telling how he'd had dinner downstairs at the bar (Caesar salad, trying to be good). He was going to catch some hockey on television and turn in early. He said he was dead tired, but he told her that he had lots of great leads on lots of great work.

He said he'd be home tomorrow.

He must have started in with everything later that night. He crushed his pills and mixed his drinks. He propped a desk chair under the door knob handle. He wrote a note and broke a lamp and crawled-stumbled into the bathroom at some point. Maybe he thought the mess would be easier. Maybe he thought about the world spinning away every time he closed his eyes.

— 2 —

Every time I come home, I'm struck by how tired and plain the town of Cargill Falls seems to me now, the streets and buildings so bleak compared to what I picture when I'm away. So much smaller than I remember. It's as if some enchantment is lifted when I return, and I can clearly see how I must have needed to make everything bigger and more important than it ever really was. That final few miles riding over the bridge above the river, past the factories, the church, the grocery and package stores, all the familiar turns I can make in my sleep, and still only an old crappy mill town.

Just a place. Nothing special or mysterious or important, yet something in how threadbare it is, something noble and sturdy in the rows of clapboard houses, the gray sidewalks, the people making their lives as best as they can. Must be the bleakness of the streets that speaks to me.

Last mile always the hardest, because I'm always wishing I could live here. It's where I belong, though even that feeling, that awareness, that desire seems fleeting. One of the last times I saw Brownie, I told him how I thought this town would have killed me if I stayed. I didn't have the constitution. I wasn't cut out for things in this place. I would never be able to survive the Elks.

199 WOODSTOCK AVENUE, and my mother has the newspaper waiting on the kitchen table. She's in her 70s now, most of her friends are gone, and she's saved the obituary. *Steven Mark Brownell died unexpectedly.* It's there in black and white, right next to the horoscopes and police reports and supermarket fliers.

We sit up late in the kitchen that night, my mother and I, and she can't let it go. How selfish he had to be to do it. All bull and no show as a man, she says, my mother just sorry for his parents, sorry for his wife and daughter, sorry for his brother and friends.

I know she's not talking about Brownie anymore. She has a box of wine in the fridge, the two of us with our jelly jars half full, my mother calling Brownie a coward.

I tell her she's not wrong. I tell her I can't defend him—or anyone else, for that matter—and I don't know what else to say.

In my childhood room, late at night, and everything is so cramped and drab compared to my memory, the room with that mothy taste. Over the years, my mother's begun using the space as storage, stacks of canned food on the desk, yard-sale chinaware and paperbacks and magazines piled on the dresser, old suitcases and boxes and folded blankets and towels on the bed. It's as if these objects have moved in and slowly taken over. It's cramped and musty in the room, and I have to clear a place for myself to sleep.

And what would someone make of the boy who once lived here, if this was all the evidence they ever knew of him? It'd be such a strange and partial glimpse of the person. It's true, no one dies without a trace, and everywhere is a tomb to unearth.

Later, at some point in the summer, Brownie's wife will get a dumpster to clean out the garage and basement. And still later, in a kind of rhyming action, I will be cleaning out my own boyhood room in order to sell the house I grew up in. I'll throw all my collections and relics unceremoniously into a dumpster. But that will be months and years away. That will be after I am done with Cargill Falls, after all of this is laid to rest.

Here and now I'm not able to sleep in this boyhood room of mine. I lie there and listen to the wind in the trees. I stare at the traffic light outside. Home, and the dark becomes a towel over my mouth. Can't quite catch a full breath.

I never asked—coward that I am—but he must have kept the secret of the gun from his mother and father all those years. I would have heard if they'd found out. I would have had to answer for what happened that day.

And as superficial as it sounds, I want to know what actually happened to the gun. But if no one is here to ask anymore, how can we ever know the truth? I could make it up—see the gun simmering in the wall with the wires and pipes, the gun patiently waiting black and cool—but there's no satisfaction in this kind of imagining. Yet what happens when you're missing things? What happens when a story is incomplete? Is it all a fiction of trees and streets in the end?

• • •

Even later, when I still can't sleep, I'll start poking around in the shelves of books from school—*Grendel, Watership Down, All Quiet, Their Eyes*—and I'll dig up some old letters from Brownie for tomorrow.

I'll be looking for props, things I can use at the Elks if all else fails: a concert ticket, a baseball card of Carlton Fisk, something from all these remains of growing up.

> *Wm—What's chiming with you? Not much here. My life has become as boring as can be. At least I'm not in trouble. Actually, I'm only bored because I have to work this week. It sucks. The working life. And you? How's that lady friend of yours? Hope I get to meet her one of these days. Should have a nice pile of dinero soon. We'll go out somewhere. Anyway, just wanted to let you know things are going pretty good.*

TODAY'S HOROSCOPE FOR LIBRA—*There are days it will all seem so random, Libra, so have faith that everything is for a reason. Conflicts over money could get in the way of your usual cordial relationships. Attention to household budget is definitely needed. You may feel your life is a great barren desert, but you will get through the crossing!*

TODAY'S HOROSCOPE FOR PISCES—*Maybe your ego isn't big enough. Is it possible that you could benefit from giving yourself more credit for the struggles you have weathered and the skills you have mastered? Take the reins, Pisces. It's up to you to change those parts of your personality that have been holding you back. Dare to be happy.*

INCOMMENSURABLE—*adj*, not able to be judged by the same standards; having no standard measurement; not commensurate <*To write a novel means to carry the incommen-*

surable to extremes in the representation of human life. (Walt. Benjamin)>; see also INADEQUATE, UNEQUAL, UNFAIR, IMMEASURABLE.

A FINAL CAUTION—*Be careful what you pick up on the battlefield. A newspaper, a can of food, and other apparently innocent articles may be "bait" for a "fool's trap," or a "booby" mine, which will explode when you pick it up.* • *Do not lay your pistol down where dirt can get into it.* • *A dirty, dry pistol, or one which has been over-oiled and allowed to gather dirt will have stoppages that may make it useless in battle, which may cost you your life.*

```
                              GENERAL
       NOTICE            WINDOW CLEANING CO.
Every signature will be confirmed
if work is satisfactorily executed.   WILLIAM LYCHACK
                                    189 Woodstock Avenue
                                    Telephone: 928-5230

                     CFalls, Conn._____ 196_
       From
                     For Window Cleaning      -   -   $
                     For Office Cleaning      -   -   $
                     For Floor Cleaning       -   -   $
                     Private Houses, window   -   -   $
                     For Building Cleaning    -   -   $
       To
                                           TOTAL  $
                     Received payment
```

They find him on a Tuesday. The memorial service is that Friday, 5 to 8 PM, upstairs hall of the Elks. Already it's crowded, cars parked along Edmond Street, and there's some kind of commotion, Brownie's father pulling out of the driveway in his truck.

"Billy Buck," he calls to me, "I'll be right back."

And he drives off.

One of his friends recognizes me and comes over to say the lights are cut off in the club. I must not understand what he means, because he explains again how the power just went down. They're sending for a ladder truck to check the transformer. It's a funny coincidence—hello, Brownie—and there's a wind through the trees, the sun setting low and warm.

No meaning to any of this, probably. Just another coincidence, but still I feel it's Brownie trying to get back at his father here. It'd be something Mr. Brownell could appreciate—CL&P, lines down, almost too perfect—how could it not be Brownie cutting the power like that? Later, I'll wonder if it was something more nuanced, something more like a hand on the shoulder of the man, less a fuck you than a little nudge to say hello.

They get the lines all sorted out in a minute, the lights flickering to life in the hall. Beneath the plaques and flags of the Elks, there's that sudden shock of small wooden chest on a table. It's the first thing I see when I walk in: blonde-wood box in a kind of spotlight, photos of Brownie in frames propped, and then Dave and Moon and Buzz and everyone else.

And here we go—Michelle and Ginny and Dawn and Donna and all the others. Brenda has a big shaky hug for me. Tommy's at the head table near the kitchen, that seasick look in his eyes, his mother sitting next to him. She doesn't seem to be seeing any of this—a glazed blankness to her—as though Brownie's mother is trying to hide her blindness. Like she can hear these people around her, but can't make out a single face.

It has the feel of a wedding, only in reverse: family sitting at the front table, Mr. Brownell with them now, portrait complete, but somehow wrong and unreal. Theirs is a grief, a distance, from which no one will return. Where did that beautiful young man from the photos go? Where even to begin?

My turn will come to say something, and I'll stand at the podium with that secret. I'll take a deep breath and try to gather what there is of myself. I'll try to say something funny, something light and hopeful. I'll say Brownie really knew how to bring people together, saying it's a lot more crowded than he would have expected.

I'll have notes for this.

I'll take them out of my pocket.

My hands at the ends of my arms will feel very far away as I carefully unfold a letter from Brownie.

To have his voice in the room, I'll read part of the letter—*what's chiming with you? just wanted to let you know things are going good*—and I'll tell how, in high school, Mr. Achtermeier would throw chalk at us if we got some piece of grammar wrong.

In English class, we sat along the windows—me, Brownie, and Dave—Mr. Achtermeier dubbing us The Zucchini Brothers. He made us laugh and we loved all his jokes and stories. There was one in particular about his father that I remember. His father had been a German sniper in the war. He'd watch through his scope as people rummaged through villages and battlefields for food. The story went how his father would shoot anyone who took a watch or ring from a body. But he would spare those who took only food or water.

Mr. Achtermeier died not long ago, I say.

You can see what kind of humor he had by going to his grave.

I have a picture.

I show the snapshot to the room.

I tell how Mr. Achtermeier always said there were three versions of the truth—your version, my version, and then The Truth. He always said that life was unfair, but it was unfair to everyone, which made life fair.

I see Dave trying to signal to me. No one knows what I'm talking about, the whole room watching speechless, this raw heart of a person talking nonsense up there, showing these pieces of Brownie to everyone, as if trying to assemble him somehow. I have Brownie's horoscope to share. I have half of a fifty-dollar bill to hold up, saying guess who had the other half?

Last but not least, I have a paperback from high school with me. I say that Brownie wasn't a big reader, but we studied this one novel together with Mr. Achtermeier back in the day, so I know he knew it. I find the page I've dog-eared, the passage that reminds me of Brownie, where Holden is telling his sister what he wants to be when he grows up—it's famous, the passage, underlined with a pen—him picturing those kids playing at the edge of some cliff, his job to catch anybody who goes over the edge. He's supposed to come out from somewhere and save them, if they're running and not looking where they're going.

Hard to recall how I get back to my seat. I say we all failed Brownie. None of us there to catch him.

—3—

Lucky for everyone, Brenda had asked Dave to say something as well, because he stands up and says what's truly required in this moment. He says how sorry he is to Mr. and Mrs. Brownell, to Tommy, to Brenda and their daughter. He says how sorry he is for their loss. That's all it takes. Good manners. Brownie deserves this. It's why we're here. It's why we're lucky to have Dave, his voice not cracking once, Dave launching into that heart-of-gold, friend-to-everyone sort of speech that all of us need to hear, a kind of best man's moment, Dave saying he doesn't mean to lay it on too thick.

Brownie could be a real fuck-up, he says, but he's sure there isn't a person in this room who doesn't have at least one good night involving the big lug, one crazy story to share, one perfect moment to hold on to.

You can hear the agreement—jostle of sound sweeping over the room, the movement of chairs, the choir of voices, the relief of laughter—and I'm so incredibly grateful to him. I'm relieved there's Dave remembering how we dropped the transmission on the Mustang one night (and there's that nod to Mr. Brownell). We drove the Cutlass into a ditch after a party at Dead End (nod to Mrs. Brownell and her car). Dave says he doesn't know much about any kids playing at the edge of a cliff (nod to me), but he asks who could forget Brownie catching for those baseball teams of ours?

Dave raises a glass. There's that music of voices, the gentle wave lifting everyone, Dave saying, "Gonna miss you, Big Guy."

I still want to tell the story of the gun. Even now, knowing better, I still feel some pivot point, those boys by the edge of the pond. I want to make sense of things. I want to find Crawford. I think I see him against the far wall. It's hard to hold onto anything. My mother is somewhere in the room, my wife and kids back home in Pittsburgh. I'm sitting at one of the tables with everyone, all of us saying how long it's been.

In the bar downstairs that night, we have a few drinks. It's the old crew. Dave, Chubs, Liz, Moon, Jen, Fritzy, Buzza. And how lucky we are to be here, remembering funny times to one another. We start in with Father Barney and CYO basketball. The girls don't seem to know the story, so we tell how every winter we had to strip down for our hernia tests.

Picture us in a line, bunch of skinny kids standing in their underwear, and Father Barney taking us one by one. He'd pluck our testicles with his fingers, good priest breathing in and out through his nose. The man's nostrils must have been stuffed with steel wool.

That steady inhale and exhale.

Like a steam engine, as we remember.

I think I can. I think I can.

He wore his collar to games and practices, as if that gave him authority. That dusting of dandruff on his shoulders, it was like he'd just returned from Santa's Village. This made his fingers extra strange, because you were bracing for ice, but then his hands were warm and soft as he instructed you to cough.

We're laughing, making funny choking noises in order to demonstrate for Jen and Liz, our palms out as if to weigh something small and delicate.

"Like a priest knows anything about hernias," I say.

"Now c'mon," says Moon, "we were lucky to have him looking out for us, keeping an eye on our testicular health."

"Right," says Dave, "big problem in youth sports back in the day."

"You never hear of hernias anymore," says Moon, "do you?"

"Because of the dedication of men like Father Barney," I say.

"You got it," says Moon.

"Who knew?" says Jen.

"Such dedication," says Liz.

"He must have loved us so much," I say.

We're around the bar, near the pool table. No music, no television, room otherwise dark and empty. We're closing down the place. Chubs comes back from the bathroom and asks what we're talking about.

"Father Barney's fingers," says Dave.

"I remember them well," says Chubs.

"There will be no casting aspersions upon Father Barney," says Moon, "may he rest in peace."

"Aspersions?" says Dave.

"Yes, aspersions, asshole," says Moon.

"Good for morale, wasn't it?" says Chubs. "Nothing like a little group molestation to really bring a team together."

"Amen," says Jen.

Moon raises a glass, "My fellow basketball brothers and sister, to Father Barney."

"Fucken perv," says Buzz.

We drink and laugh, and Dave brings another round for everyone on a tray. Shots of Jäeger for old times' sake. We toast Brownie. We toast Mr. Achtermeier. We toast Cathy.

Liz says that her very first date was with Brownie. "We went with you and Michelle," she says to me.

"I remember sitting there next to Steve," she says to everyone. "He had his big cozy arm plopping heavily around my shoulder. Must have been such a tough way to sit for two hours."

And just when the room gets to seem too quiet, the door pushes open, Crawford striding in with his wife, everyone cheering. He looks young, and we make room, get them seats, hugs all around, Crawford tall and lanky and easy in his movements, his wife lovely and smiling. We say we were just reminiscing, remembering those hernia tests with Father Barney.

"Good times," says Crawford. "As long as we don't have to relive them."

Moon reaches over and says, "Just a little cough, please."

And Crawford swats his hand, saying get the fuck out of here, everyone laughing. There's another round for the table, and we catch each other up on the last twenty, the last thirty years. Crawford has snapshots of his two boys in his wallet, handsome kids, proud papa. The whole night slides by, everyone laughing and wistful and alive, and soon we'll be gone.

• • •

I'll still want to tell the story of the gun. I'll still feel for those boys by the edge of the pond, as if this was the one place, the one chance they had to make sense of things.

The trouble is the gun doesn't explain anything. It never did, and it never will. There's no connection, no shadow to understand, nothing to forgive or lay to rest. Try to read one in terms of the other all you want, but the gun never touches the suicide in any way in the end. Which means it can be lifted away, finally, the gun turning out to be absolutely nothing. Those boys, those two numbskulls, they can go free.

No more Brownie.

He's ashes now.

And no more Mouse, either.

There's the father that I am to my children, the husband I am to my wife, the teacher, the guy who was good at school, bad at bartending. And the real mystery is how anyone finds their way forward in all of this. How does someone who feels so stuck and lost keep going? How can he necessitate all the many accidents that befall him? How can a person learn to be good—good most of the time, at least, or maybe just enough of the time?

In another life—there are, it turns out, many lives in this one existence of ours—I am someone who ends up going to Myanmar to be a Buddhist monk. This, too, is like a dream, no need for explanation, but at my ordination I am given a new name, U Sâsana. I go and live for a time in a forest monastery on the southern Shan plateau.

I will talk about this in my classes back home. I will explain how the Buddhists have this idea of original suffering. This is something you carry with you your whole life. It's not always obvious to you what the suffering is—or sometimes it's so obvious you don't count it as anything—but every choice you make can be traced back to this one thing, your giftcurse, your entire character stemming from this.

More than once, I will go to be a monk. It will be as far from home as I can get. The antipode, the complete opposite side of the world in every way. When asked why, I'll explain to friends how I must have been here as a Burman in a previous life. A Burman, or a Brit, someone with a great affinity for his station here, someone who found he loved the heat and rain, someone who could go as if by memory along certain roads and rivers. This will make about as much sense as anything to my Burmese friends.

For them it is enough to say you simply feel drawn to a place.

No need to spell out such yearning.

In Myanmar, if you pass unsatisfied from this life, you are reborn on the plane of hungry ghosts, your soul coming back again to complete some piece of unfinished business. As they say, it took the Buddha many lives to become the Buddha. With this in mind, it is possible to have empathy for someone going back and forth over a particular piece of ground, as if trying to find something they have lost, as if trying to lift some curse they have been under.

One afternoon, driving in our jeep from Mandalay to Yangon, we stop at a roadside gas station. There's a small village nearby, and off to the side a very old woman is selling teak chocks. They're used as parking brakes for cars and trucks, these fresh-cut wedges stacked in all sizes around her. She's no bigger than a small boy, this woman inviting us to sit with her in the shade. She offers tea and mangoes. The air is pleasant off the small pond behind the house. She wants to know the story of us: our heads shaved clean, we explain that we've just left the monastery in the forest, just been disrobed, on our way back now to the jungle of the real world. She's pleased and tells how she's lived never far from this hill her entire life.

We're only there for ten minutes—the space of a cup of tea, the engine of our Jeep ticking itself cool nearby— and she relights her cheroot and tells of her children, her grandchildren, her husband's death, and how she laughed at her younger brother when she was six years old. She didn't know any better, the boy in his coffin in the front room of the house, but almost ninety years after the fact she's still known in the village as the girl who couldn't stop giggling at her brother's funeral. It's alive in her face, the sadness and shame, the acceptance, the odd, enduring sense of identity.

Of all the stories she could have told, *that* was the one she chose. That must mean something. Of all the things that survived, all the things she might have wanted us to know, it was that single moment from a lifetime, this young girl reacting to the sight of her brother lying there as if asleep.

— 4 —

Before anything bad can happen—before the gun, before the dog, before all the crap that would come cluttering into this life—there are these kids out on the pond. It's winter vacation, and my friend is on his way to my house. I'll watch for him to appear along the cemetery wall. My mother has stretched cellophane over the windows, the plastic making it feel as if the house is going blind, everything blurry as I watch from the kitchen for Brownie.

We're on our way to the pond. We're ten years old and the air slips straight through my coat, our boots crunching over the frozen grass of the cemetery, hockey sticks and skates over our shoulders. It's not even Christmas, and yet it's record-book cold, cold like the Old Country, cold like you read about.

The ice is more than thick enough for us to skate. (Brownie's father was here earlier in the week to make sure, it being so soon in the season, the man finding even the dam frozen, whole spillway encased.) And it has not yet begun to snow, either. Just this dry Arctic freeze, this low pressure pressing down from Canada, this beautiful clarity sitting over us for days.

And the day will be, in its own way, absolutely perfect. Not a cloud in the sky, no snow on the ground, everything vivid, everything sharp and close and clean in the light, the whole world crystalized. It's the kind of day that makes you feel you've been missing something, missing just how precise and profound every detail can be, if only you can open your eyes. There's a taste of pines toward the back of the cemetery, a hint of wood smoke, voices in the distance, and then the most unbelievable ice on the pond, silvery white in the sun, smooth as a mirror.

The ice is flawless.

No ruts, no cracks, kids out there playing tag. It's pristine and beautiful. You can hear the blades—the strokes like long sheets of paper being torn—and there's a campfire going, a circle of logs and stones where we change into our skates.

Brownie has those skates with the quick-release clasps, so he's on the ice first, him gliding out there smooth and graceful. He can do anything he wants on those blades—forward, backward, edges sharp as scissors—while my own laces take forever to tighten, even with that little metal hook I carry. I am still getting ready when Brownie comes back to dump his coat by our shoes, his bangs pinned with sweat.

I suddenly remember the sandwiches that my mother made for us back home. I tell him I forgot our lunch and thermos of hot chocolate. He says we'll survive, Brownie back to the ice, calling for me to hurry up.

"C'mon," he says, "let's get out there already!"

• • •

A bunch of us discover that the brook feeding into the pond has frozen. There's a couple of open patches you have to walk around, but deeper into the woods the little stream is pure glass. This is us flying past the trees. It's us as wolves on the hunt, seven or eight in a pack, whole string of us slicing through the forest.

Sometimes there's a false floor of glazing over the real ice—a loud electric sizzle, like we're riding trolley wires, a rain of sparks cascading behind—and it's glorious, small licks of talc swirling down through shafts of light. We howl to the woods. We jump a fallen tree. Openings of dark water appear at the fast-moving drops in the stream, and we get down on our bellies and dip our faces to drink, the water so crystal cold and satisfying, flecks of gold in the bottom gravel, that mentholated cool on our cheeks and mouths as we skate deeper into the woods.

There are places where the brook separates and comes back together, little islands, forks in the path, and we keep following these narrow cuts of frozen water. I'm not half as fast as everyone else. Scottie, Marla, Laura, Raymond, Joey, all of them better on skates. So it's fine to let Brownie and the rest of them pull away. It's fine to be alone in the woods.

There are stone walls out here, which means the trees were all once cleared, land once used as pasture. There's a brick chimney standing in the middle of nowhere, kind of spooky, kind of haunted. An open well waits as a trap. We all know these things. We were born to this place. It's completely ours. No one will ever appreciate it better.

I coast along on my skates—slow and easy—the ice so clear it's not even there. Eventually I stop and lie down and rest on the brook. It's a glass-bottom boat under me, faint circuitry of water burbling under the surface, sunlight like coins falling through the trees. I numb my cheek against that burn of ice and watch the flow of weeds underneath. The long green hair of a girl in the wind. I'm nowhere to be found. I could stay here my whole life.

In all my time on earth, this is what it is to feel alive on a good day, the whole universe full and beautiful and worthy of awe. Everything will be good in this moment, including me, including all of us in this place together.

Can never be sure how long such a moment will last, but I'll take lying on that stream for just a bit more. Why not? Who can stop me? Is there anywhere else I would rather be? Is there any place better?

I can lie here forever, just waiting for the gradual sound of skates coming back to find me—*sharks, sharks, sharks*—it's Brownie skating bigger and bigger toward where I am. Who else could it be?

I'll let him discover whatever is here sprawled out on the ice. I'll want him to laugh when he sees me. And that shearing gets closer, Brownie in the woods, moving fast and happy and full of confidence, his face flushed and bright, this boy with his whole life in front of him.

It's from here—this is the spot from which we'll want to start over—Brownie still scrawny compared to what he'll become, neither of us close to filling out our bodies, and me his best friend in the world. There I am, just grinning up from the middle of the stream, that fine spray of ice as he stops within an inch of my life, Brownie saying, "Isn't this all so amazing?"

ACKNOWLEDGEMENTS:

I am beyond grateful—one could say profoundly moved—to be blessed with so many friends who helped to see me through this project. In particular, this book could not have been written without Mike Paterniti, Miles Harvey, Kate McQuade, Geeta Kothari, Michael Lowenthal, and Glenn Stowell. Thanks go as well to Cindy House, Dave Cullen, Tony Ward, Cammie McGovern, Sherrie Flick, Chris Lynch, Kelly Chastain, Craig Bernier, Kevin O'Connor, Peter Trachtenberg, Jeanne Marie Laskas, Mike Meyer, Jeff Oaks, Don Bialostosky, and Marly Rusoff. Huge thanks to Jeff Condran and Robert Peluso for making a home for this novel, and to Gretchen Koss for helping the book find its way. It goes without saying, but thank you once again, Betty. TLID—The Love Is Deep—and runs to you, Frederick, William, and Burgess. Thanks, finally, to those lifelong friends from home: Dave, Liz, Jon, Crawf, Jen, Chubs, Moon, Buzz, Brenda... You're all in here... Should have at least changed our names... But then again, as Dave asked, "Do you think anyone outside our little town will really care about any of this?"

William Lychack lives in Pittsburgh, Pennsylvania, and teaches at the University of Pittsburgh. His work has appeared in *The Best American Short Stories, The Pushcart Prize,* and on public radio's *This American Life.* He is the author of five previous books, including a novel, *The Wasp Eater*, a collection of stories, *The Architect of Flowers*, a cultural history of cement, and two children's books.

More can be found at www.lychack.com.

Author photo by Yan Naing Htun.

CPSIA information can be obtained
at www.ICGtesting.com
Printed in the USA
FSHW011836191219